Mana

The Magic Beyond The Rainbow

Maria Cowen

TABLE OF CONTENTS

PART ONE:
GETTING THERE

1

In the last-minute flurry of events and misadventures surrounding his high school graduation Robert Radcliffe had major misgivings about ever getting through all the pomp and ceremony in one piece, and on with his life. But he'd finally made it to LAX on the appointed day. He shifted his weight uncomfortably and hefted his backpack into a new position as he stood in the check-in line and thought how good it felt to be free, really and truly free from boring schoolwork and parental supervision. Not that he minded his mom and pop.

They were terrific people who loved him a lot. But sometimes they treated him like he was still in diapers practically and mom still called him her baby. Ha! Little did she know how much her baby enjoyed groping the girls under their beach towels after a good day of surfing at Malibu!

This backpacking trip abroad had been on his

agenda ever since his sophomore year at John Marshall High, when his grades badly needed a transfusion and his parents cut a deal with him that promised a full summer of travel if he could manage to graduate with a 3.5 average or better. Well, he'd made it and here he was waiting to board United Flight 987 to Honolulu.

"Hawaii? What a blast!" some friends had screeched with envy, while others thought he should be backpacking through Europe, or Australia, or the Amazon, instead. It had been tough to choose between all the world's exciting foreign destinations, and his room had been littered with travel brochures and geographical picture books for the better part of his senior year.

But, finally, it came to him that he wanted a destination where he could speak the language, one that was tropical, had jungles to explore, and where beautiful primitive fauna and virgin flora could be captured by the lens of his fabulous new Nikon, a graduation gift from Uncle Roy. At first he'd decided on the South Pacific. Names like Tonga, Tahiti, Fiji and Bora Bora evoked exotic passages from books he'd read. But his parents had counseled him away from the South Pacific because of certain areas of political unrest.

In general, the people he'd talked to had been in favor of Hawaii. Once the home of Robert Louis Stevenson, beloved by James Michener, it was still the prettiest string of pearls in any man's ocean according to his English teacher who moved into his time-sharing condo on Maui every summer like clockwork.

His Biology instructor had seconded the motion, extolling the beauties of the coral reefs, the powdery whiteness of the sandy beaches, and the exuberantly lush foliage to be found in remote areas of the Big Island or on Kauai. Some of his buddies had spent summers with their parents on Maui and Oahu where they gave rave notices to those places as a surfer's paradise.

Despite his mother's urging that he take an economy round trip package with room and car on every island, Robert had insisted on a round trip ticket and a book of traveler's checks. Nothing more. What did he want with fancy hotel reservations and pre-packaged tours? He stubbornly stuck to his ideal of going where the wind blew him and promised to fire off a post card from every stop he made, just so the family wouldn't worry although he knew mom would worry about her baby, even if he were traveling with Chuck Norris for a chaperone!

His buddies thought he was crazy to travel alone into the jungle when he could sit by the pool of a big hotel and eyeball the bikinis instead, or catch a wave on the Banzai Pipeline.

They teased him about it as they waited by the airport curb while he hopped out of the old restored Desoto classic convertible owned by his best friend Ralston Howard. He was glad the whole bunch had come to see him off, and equally relieved to see no one made a move to enter the airport with him. Ral, alone, understood Robert's need to follow his dream. Ral was the only one he would read to from his journal when he got back in August.

He shifted his weight again and then decided to unbuckle the heavy oversized backpack as he waited in the United departure lounge. Thanks to a shopping foray with his dad into L.A.'s biggest sporting goods emporium, he was loaded with all the survival gear he could carry, including field glasses, a sleeping bag, mosquito netting, one-man tent, propane stove and tank, water canteen, freeze-dried food, trail mix and cooking utensils.

Then there were the little necessities like his iPod, writing kit, first-aid kit, camera, lots of film, changes of clothing' and self-seal baggies for collecting specimens. His hiking boots were too bulky to pack, so he wore them, along with walking shorts and bush jacket. More than a few curious passengers turned to stare as he shrugged out of the straps and lowered the bulky pack in one of the plastic shell chairs and himself into another.

***

2

The five-hour flight to Honolulu was passed in unbroken boredom. They were showing a fairy lousy film, so he wasn't disturbed by the fact that he couldn't see the screen from his seat. After twirling the dial in vain to find some decent rock music, Robert returned his earphones to the hostess in disgust and asked for a refund, a blanket and a pillow which he promptly got. He spent the rest of the flight trying to corkscrew his lanky body into some sort of position which would invite sleep. Obviously, economy class seats offered little in the way of comfort for by the time they came in for a smooth landing on the Reef Runway in Honolulu his muscles were severely cramped and aching.

Blinking as he stumbled out onto the top step of the

planes exit ramp, Robert pulled on his polarized glasses and looked around as he began his descent. What he beheld banished all the stiffness and cramps from his mind, as he was greeted by clear blue skies, puffy little white cotton ball clouds, stately palms and colorful bougainvillea spilling out of the planter boxes and landscaping. This looked like paradise all right.

The moment he walked out of the plane a blanket of hot, moist air enveloped him and threatened to stifle his breathing. The humidity was nothing he'd ever encountered before in his life, it tickled his skin and caused him to break out in profuse perspiration within seconds of his exposure to it.

Jeez, where were those trade winds the tourist pamphlets all crowed about? Just another dose of media hype, he decided. Nevertheless, his heart did a little flip-flop of anticipation as he descended the boarding ramp and strode across the tarmac towards a sign that read Arrivals Honolulu International Airport, and under it Passenger.

Hooking his thumbs under the sturdy shoulder straps of his pack, Robert weaved through the crowds, avoided the baggage claim area and made his way past smiling hula girls with carnation leis who were being herded around by a tour guide in search of the newest malihini group arrivals. He spotted the SIDA Taxi stand by the curb. Several SIDA cars were lined up, their windows rolled down to catch the slightest whiff of breeze.

The winds were blowing Kona today and the kamaaina, drivers knew, until the trades came back, there would be no relief in sight. All of them wore matching aloha shirts of white trimmed with a bright floral print in primary colors, and none of them seemed the slightest bit interested in the visitors emerging from the terminal. It seemed right, somehow, to see the cabbies reading or snoozing lazily on this muggy afternoon. Then he realized why. The dispatcher appeared from out of nowhere and blew shrilly on her whistle, motioning for the lead cab to pull ahead into the loading zone and pick up a waiting family of haole visitors.

Shrugging off his backpack, Robert lowered it to the sidewalk and motioned to the dispatcher that he needed a cab, too. She nodded officiously and walked over to him, pencil poised above a clipboard and pad. "Where to?" No Aloha greeting. She was all business. Oh, well. If he'd wanted leis and alohas, he could have taken his mother's advice, and her recommended package tour.

He felt disappointed. The tourist folders said aloha was in the spirit of the island people. Was it, more accurately, just another commodity sold to visitors for the right price? "I don't have reservations," he replied. "You can get one. Go to the bank of hotel phones over there," she pointed with her clipboard in the general direction of a wall inside the terminal and pivoted to leave.

"Wait, Miss. I don't want a reservation, sight-unseen. I want to pick my own hotel in person. Can the driver just drop me off in Waikiki?" "Try wait?" she said in pidgin. Then she leaned into the next cab in line. "Howzit, Primo. Dis kid, he no got hotel. Take him Waikiki. He like walk around, to find da kine by hisself." The driver hoisted himself out of the cab and opened the trunk, eyeing Robert suspiciously as he lowered his pack carefully into the compartment.

To Primo's jaded eyes, the boy was just another weird-looking mainland tourist, over-dressed and under-experienced. He could always spot the akamai travelers. They wore lightweight cotton clothing, flip-flops and carried a small overnight bag in contrast to the polyester-suited, slightly sloshed first-time tourist with too much matching luggage.

This kid looked like he got on the wrong plane. All he lacked was a pith helmet and a ticket to Africa. Primo coughed to hide a smirk. Robert was thankful when the power windows were rolled up and the driver turned on the air. "You like take Freeway or Nimitz?" Primo asked into his rear view mirror, "What's Nimitz?" Robert asked.

"Nimitz go by waterfront and downtown. Mo'bettah scenic way." Primo's version of the English language left a great deal to be desired, but Robert was slowly getting the hang of it. "Waterfront way, please" he replied. The ride was all too brief, however, and in fifteen minutes he found himself cruising past a shopping center, a canal, some condos, a boat basin and a big hotel with a rainbow colored mosaic covering the whole side of one building.

He knew instinctively that they had arrived in the concrete jungle of Waikiki. "Excuse me, driver. Is this Waikiki?" "Mo'bettah you call me Primo. Yeah, but Waikiki still yet ovah deah." He pointed to even more high-rise condos. "We go Kalakaua way, and you see. You tell me wheah you like stop. Den I stop."

Manipulating his way through crushing traffic three lanes deep. Primo turned past Fort De Russy and onto Saratoga for the block that led into Kalakaua. Robert was growing more alarmed by the minute. The more they drove, the more concrete he saw. The street was lined with glittering hotels, boutiques and wide sidewalks swarming with thousands of milling tourist couples wearing matching polyester leis.

Two-fer outfits. His aloha shirt matched her muumuu and plastic flower. Robert was aghast. "Primo. This looks more like Holly-weird than paradise. I think I'm in the wrong place...I" "Holly-weird? Hey, dat's funny. I nevah been went to Hollywood, but I can guarantee you're in Waikiki, my friend." Robert gave his driver the once-over while he reflected on what to do next.

The guy was real small, not quite five feet tall, and his olive drab, grainy skin was pulled taut over a fragile frame that looked like it needed a few good home-cooked meals. It was impossible to tell how old the guy might be and, with his crooked grin, jug-ears and funny way of talking, he sure was a comical sight. "Hey, Primo. What I meant was, this place might be great for some people, but I came here to find a more natural retreat. You know, a place with trees, mountains, waterfalls and secluded beaches."

"Ah. I get you. My home stay on da island of Kauai, ant we still have unexplored country d'ere, on da Na Pali coast, paradise for real!" "No kidding!" Robert turned an eager smile toward his little driver. "I was wondering where you were from. Are you a real Hawaiian?" Primo threw his head back and laughed merrily, flashing rows of worn gold crowns on his molars. "Local boy, yeah. But no Hawaiian. I descend from people of MU."

Robert's uncomprehending expression caused the little man to pause and explain. "You probably no stay informed about da race of MU in yo' fancy history books. My people sailed from Polynesia wit original settlers to dese islands. Da Mu work lak servants or slaves. Today, not many MU left anymol. Almos' extinct, like ancient volcanoes on Kauai, we are."

"Wow! Are you full-blooded MU, Primo?"

"Yeah. I stay pure MU kine."

"Are all your people small, like you?"

"Yeah, I guess. Some smaller, tho'." The little man tilted his comical head at Robert and surprised him with his next remark, "I tell you one good place to go, it is called Na Pali. You can climb da jungle trail to high cliffs overlooking Na Pali Coast wilderness."

Holy Moley, the little guy was reading his mind! "You mean I should go to your home island? What did you call it, Cow-eve?"

"Ho! You are typical haole tourist kid. Try say Cow-everee."

"Okay, Primo. Is it on Cowreyeree?"

"Sure. Just up da coast from Hanalei. My grandad he still live deah.

Real paradise ovah deah, like in Hawaii of old times," "How would I get there?"

"Fly! No mo' dan twenty minute away. Den drive up da coast to Hanalei an visit my grandad. He can show you da hiking trail."

Robert had read about Kauai in the tourist folders, it was called the Garden Isle. Sounded very promising. "Okay, Primo, where do I get a reservation for Cow-eve-ee." "No problem! I drive you right back to airport.

Flights go every half hour, easy. Look," he scribbled on a grubby match folder, "I give you address of old Moki, my granddad. You say hello fo' me wen you get dere." He flashed his toothy golden grin again as he headed for McCully Street and the entrance onto the freeway.

***

3

The Hawaiian Air flight landed on Kauai before Robert had a chance to finish the plastic glass of fruit punch which was served to him by an adorable oriental hostess. No great loss, since he'd never liked fruit punch all that much anyway.

The Lihue airport was dramatically empty in contrast to the madhouse he had left behind at Honolulu International. It sat on a spit of land near the ocean, a layer of reddish dust covering its shellacked line of low bungalows, sleeping in the noonday sun.

There wasn't much action either inside or outside of the terminal. He sat on a bench and sipped at a soda from the machine while he wrote his first post card back home. At least they know he arrived safely. Across a divided driveway Robert spotted a row of car rental booths and strolled over to ask if there was any public bus service available. He struck out. No busses. Turned out the big hotels ran their own private transfer services for a hefty price. Great!

Robert shoved his hands in his pockets and paced the sidewalk, trying to think what to do next. Oh sure, he could rent a car for a few bucks a day but it would probably get stolen while he was hiking through the jungle. He could see it now. Panic city. Police reports. Alarming his parents. Nope. Forget that. No car rental.

He looked up and that's when he saw it. It literally took his breath away. Over towards the mountains. There it was. A triple rainbow! God, he'd never seen anything like it in his life! Three rainbows dazzling radiant against an aquarelle sky. He was glad he was on a field trip with his art class, he'd never be able to do it justice. Just then he remembered his camera which was hanging from his neck and snapped off the lens cover to focus on the panorama. Now he'd need a super-wide-angle lens to take it all in. Damn! He'd have to settle for two shots, putting half the triple rainbow in each one.

His absorption with photographing the rainbows had attracted the attention of a young honeymooning couple from Minnesota, who soon joined him to try for some photos of their own. They struck up a conversation and asked Robert to photograph them on their camera with the rainbows in the background. He learned Brian and Brenda had rented a car and would be honeymooning in a condo at Princeville.

When they in turn asked where he would be staying and he mentioned Hanalei, they exclaimed that they would all be going in the same direction and offered him a ride. He looked it up in This Week in Kauai, the handout tourist brochure. Yes, they were right. Hanalei was Just Past Princeville! He accepted with alacrity, pressing a five dollar bill into Brian's hand to help with the gas, and together they started off.

The drive through old Lihue town was mildly interesting, but did not draw their attention enough to stop. But once they had passed the hotels on the east shore and entered open country, they began to really feel they were in a place apart. The rolling foothills were so green and the vegetation so beautiful, it looked as if it had been planned by a master gardener. The miles rolled on unbroken except for a stop here and there at a coastal scenic lookout and the detour to the Old Lighthouse and an Avian Preserve.

Time slipped by and the afternoon drew to a close. As they neared Princeville, Brian decided it would be better to drive ahead to Hanalei as Robert would never reach his destination before dark if he was left on the highway to hitch another ride. Before another half hour had passed, they were in Hanalei, and Robert and his new friends bid a somewhat reluctant goodbye to each other in front of the antiquated sundries store.

***

4

Walking inside, he was surprised by the gloom. He spied an old crone of a woman seated behind the counter and cleared his throat. "Ahemmm. Ma'am. Good afternoon. I wonder if you could direct me to the house of old Moki." "Moki? Ha! He don't get many visitors these days. What you want Moki for?

"I bring greetings from his grandson, Primo, in Honolulu."

"Ah so in that case, take da narrow dirt road behind die store and go mauka to foot of da pali. Moki's house is da last one." "Mauka? Pali?

"Mauka, boy toward da mountain. Pali, da volcanic ridge! You must you no can understand. Malihini one stranger to desert islands but you brown enuf to look Portugee. You go now, Boy. I close up now." She wagged a stern finger at him. Robert stifled a laugh. She was an old softie, he could tell. "Yes Ma'am, thank you for the directions.

"No say thank you, Boy. Say talk Hawaiian kine." Mahalo! You are in Hawaii so now you kine. He'd heard that before, and he wondered what it meant. But he dared not offend her by asking for more translations. He'd heard too. And at least he knew that it meant thanks. Oh, yes, Mahalo before, Mahalo, Ma'am."

"Dey call me Tutu. You call me Tutu too, since you friend of Primo and Moki. Now go! Aloha!" She shooed him out the door and bolted it before shuffling off down the street.

Robert followed instructions and arrived at the last house at the foot of the mountain just as the last rays of the sun slanted through the trees. He approached the ramshackle old cabin cautiously. It appeared vacant. "Just my luck", he thought, there's nobody home after I've come all this way. He was glad he had his camping gear on his back. Then a movement caught his eye in one of the windows and he turned to look just as a completely bald head disappeared from view. "Hello!" he called. "Hello! Is anybody home?"

"Who are you? Why you spy on me?" demanded the ancient wrinkled figure that had reappeared in the doorway. His ears looked like Primo's, but that was where the resemblance ended. The rest of him looked like a frail, overgrown, tail-less monkey. Two black, beady eyes glowered at the tall, tangy, dark-haired young man suspiciously. I just dropped in to bring you a greeting from your grandson, Primo, but I can see that you do not welcome visitors, so I'll leave. Goodbye, Mister Moki."

The old man's face suddenly transformed into a huge grin. "Primo? You friend of Primo? I no see my grandson since he went stay O'ahu to make his fortune. Come in, young man. Come in! I lak hear all about my grandson. I lak hear about da big city of Honolulu!" He moved across the distance between them with surprising speed for one so ancient, and pulled the astonished Robert into his cabin. "I was about to have my suppah. You will eat wit' me and we will talk, eh? Eh? Now, lay down yo' stuff and sit."

Robert lowered his backpack to the floor and propped it beside the door frame, then he followed the old man's beckoning hand to the kitchen and seated himself at the table while Moki ladled out a plate of spicy, aromatic stew and set it before him.

Robert was a little embarrassed. He felt like a fraud, accepting old Moki's hospitality when he could lay no claim to a friendship with Primo and even less to any knowledge of Honolulu. But the old man must have been starved for company because he entertained Robert with stories until Robert could hold his eyes open no longer and the old man invited him to throw his bedroll on the floor and stay the night.

Morning came, and the smell of strong coffee stung his nose and reminded him where he was. But when he tried to roll out of the sleeping bag his bones protested. How could he feel so stiff after such a sound, dreamless sleep? He hoped the soft jungle carpet would be kinder to his body than Moki's old plank floor had been.

At breakfast, Robert explained the purpose of his visit to old Moki, who listened patiently and then offered to take him to the Na Pali hiking trail. "Moki, any advice you can give me will be very much appreciated. Have you ever climbed the Na Pali yourself? "Many time, young man. Many time I go. Da only access to Na Pali coast is on foot. I make da climb many time when I was boy like you. One time I stay up deah for too-tree wiks."

"Great! Then you can tell me where to go, what not to do, and all that kind of thing!" "Yeah, I will tell. You must no go near Menehune. Menehune are humbug. One time, I see da Menehune ant I get veeery bad luck. Some people stick aroun' dem ant go crazy' act lolo" He rapped on his skull for emphasis. But udderwise you will find no danger. No poison kine plants, insects or reptiles in dis jungle. Only danger is Menehune. You be careful!"

After breakfast, Robert loaded his pack into the back of Moki's old pickup and they drove, creaking and rattling to Tutu's store to buy some canned sodas, chocolate bars and other last-minute stuff. Then Moki steered his battered old rust bucket down the highway until it branched off and wound around the base of the mountains for several miles.

When the road came to the end, Moki gave Robert an impulsive hug around the waist, which was as high as he could reach and said, "Robert, you come my place, visit again when your climb is pau. Okay?" "Okay, Moki. I promise I'll come and visit you on the way back." Ea!! There was another one of those words! He wished he'd thought to stop and buy a dictionary of the local jargon, if such a thing even existed. Sometimes these people seemed to be talking another language!

***

5

Robert unsnapped a pouch on his pack and pulled out a Hiking Guide to Kauai, which he'd found in the airport magazine shop. Showing it reassuringly to Moki, he waved and started off along the trail. It was comforting to know Kauai's jungles were harmless and unpopulated by man eating animals. He just prayed Moki was right about there not being any scorpions or snakes. Upward he walked.

The trail was well defined and the shrubbery was thick and exotic with little waterfalls trickling along here and there. After a couple of hours his pack was starting to feel like it was loaded with cement building blocks and he could feel the blisters blossoming inside his stiff hiking boots. "Oh, come of it, Rob," he growled aloud to himself. "Self-pity gets you nowhere. Stiff upper lip and forward march. You wanted to explore the tropical jungle and that's just what you're going to do!"

He trudged along for another fifteen minutes, looking constantly at his watch. The time was dragging by. His feet were throbbing inside the sweaty, rigid boots and his jacket was soaked through. For the first time he suspected that maybe he was not properly dressed. Listen, friend, he coached himself, you wanted adventure, didn't you? Did you think this was going to be Sunday afternoon in the park? No, Sir. You won't find adventure without testing your endurance! Press adventure, press on, Rob, Press on! He shifted his backpack for the umpteenth time and lurched upward, whistling in an effort to ignore his discomfort.

The sun was still high and it filtered down through the misty canopy of pines and banyans to the ferns and elephant ear vines below. It was beautiful, like a dream forest with the birds calling and darting from tree to tree high overhead.

Robert shrugged out of his pack and sat on a mossy bank with his back to a big tree. He unlaced his shoes, removing them to gingerly examine his blister bubbles and fished around for the tin of Band-Aids to apply to the sores. Then he pulled out a bag of trail mix and a soft drink for lunch, pausing occasionally to raise his camera and record the changing light and shadow patterns on the foliage. He judged that he must have climbed several thousand feet above sea level, as he could already see the misty cliffs of the Na Pali Coast. What secrets would they reveal to him?

Well, my friend, if you ever win the war with these boots, you might just make it all the way up there and find your answer, he smiled and stretched out for a quick nap, setting the alarm on his wristwatch and using his bulky pack for a pillow.

***

6

Robert awoke, refreshed, and opened his eyes to the surprise of an exquisite green dragonfly dipping and swooping around his head. The cool green moss had conformed to his aching bones and the banyan he was resting under provided a soft dappled shade. What a pity he couldn't make camp right here in this terrific place.

He spread his Hiker's Guide out on the mossy ground and fished in the pack for his canteen and a stick of chewing gum. The water was lukewarm, but it freshened his parched lips and eased the dryness in his throat. The stick of chewing gum tasted good, and made his mouth feel sweet again.

Sweet enough to kiss, he thought bemusedly, as he let a vision of Tessa, his blonde girlfriend, run through his mind in her bikini. Tessa's bouncy, golden curls contrasted with Robert's dark tumble of hair, her pint and gold tan with his lean and muscular bronze, Tessa said he was a real babe and her girlfriends thought she was the flukiest girl in John Marshall High, to have lucked out on him.

He realized he was fantasizing and wiped the silly grin off his face. Hadn't he planned this trip in order to get the smog out of his brain and do some serious self-exploration before he headed into college and began to make the decisions' about life and love, that would affect the rest of his life?

It looked as if he still had a couple of miles to walk before he reached the campsite indicated on the map. He knew that in a state-controlled wilderness park you couldn't just pitch camp where you damned well pleased. You had to play by the rules. Pity, he was comfortable enough right where he was. Half an hour later, he passed Brian and Brenda hiking downhill.

They wore hiking boots and backpacks, but were

otherwise stark, raving naked! Robert blinked in disbelief, then looked again. Either his eyes were deceiving him or his mind was playing tricks. He wondered if he'd had too much sun. Weren't they supposed to be staying at Princeville? "Hi there!" the girl greeted him with a friendly wave, apparently unembarrassed by his obvious stare. Her evenly tanned young body glistened with Suntan Oil. Her companion wore his hair in long, angelic curls which fell to his shoulders and looked at Robert challengingly. He quickly averted his eyes from the girl.

"Oh, hi! Small world. Do you know how far it is from here to the camp site?" He tried to sound casual. "Not far. Just another few minutes' walk." the girl replied. "You should hurry and pitch your camp, thought it'll be dark soon," added her angelic-looking partner.

"Say, you two. Don't laugh. I almost didn't recognize you without your clothes, but you look just like Brian and Brenda, the couple I rode up to Hanalei with..." Robert began, but trailed off when the couple disappeared into the lush vegetation of the trail as though they had not heard him speak. Nudity was nothing new to Robert. Had gone skinny dipping after weenie roasts at Malibu, and there's been other assorted events at parties, even a mooning once that nearly got him and F and expelled. But this confrontation shook him more profoundly than he was willing to admit. He couldn't help wondering what might have transpired if he'd met the shapely young woman hiking alone.

His imagination took over as he trudged along fantasizing his own erotic variations. *"Hey, Rob! Don't waste your time with impossible ideas,"* a voice scolded inside his head. Then he remembered there was reputed to be a nudist colony down in Hanakoa Valley, and laughed. Suddenly he was not confused by the encounter anymore. Thank goodness, he thought. I was almost convinced I'd been imagining things!

The first few drops of rain hinted at a pending cloudburst and all thoughts of erotica vanished in the urgency to find cover before he, and his provisions, got soaked.

He yanked his tent out from the backpack and quickly set it up in a small cave-like hollow he found in an outcropping of the lava rocks. The location offered ideal shelter from rain and wind. He pushed his pack inside the tent and tossed his jacket in after it. Just in time. He wondered if this area was within camping limits. Too bad if it wasn't. He'd just have to take his chances and hope a park ranger wouldn't come along and make him move.

It was still spitting so he decided to light his propane stove and cook himself some dinner before the night and the rains came. By seven o'clock he was sitting in the doorway of his tent with a cup of instant coffee in one hand and a pot of canned meat balls in stew between his legs, spooning it hungrily into his mouth. This is the life, he thought, as he bit into a meatball and let the tomato sauce drip off his chin.

He ate too fast. He could feel the heartburn already. His mother's voice came to him, scolding sweetly as she prepared an Alka-Seltzer. He rummaged in his first-aid kit and came up with some antacid tabs. Popping two in his mouth, he crawled outside and folded the camp stove, storing it inside his tent. None too soon.

He was head-in, tail-outside the tent organizing his gear when he felt as though somebody had dumped a bucket of water on his rear end. He quickly moved inside and lowered the flap. The deluge was heavy and there seemed no letup in sight. Robert lit his lantern and studied his Hiker's Guide for a while. Then he found the post cards he'd bought at the Lihue airport and scribbled messages to everyone whose address he remembered.

The rain pounded down as though it would never stop. He stuffed the post cards back inside his pack and crawled into his sleeping bag. It was pitch black outside and his aching muscles told him it was time to close his eyes and get some rest. Tomorrow he hoped the rain would vaporize in the dawn of a tropical, hot new day.

***

7

Robert woke up with a start. The luminous dial on his watch read 3:50 a.m. Then he heard it. Something was moving out there! Holding his breath, he tensed and listened as the hair on his arms stood on end. At first all he heard was the dripping of water off the foliage and onto his tent. He carefully pushed open the flap and peered out. The night was black as ink, with no moon shining through the dense cloud cover. Then he heard it again. Voices, whispering rapidly, followed by muffled laughter and the rustle of running feet through the grass.

Some campers must be having a party somewhere nearby, he thought to himself with relief. And yet something nagged at the edge of his mind. Like when he'd see those pictures that were captioned, find what's out of place in this sketch, and it would turn out there was a rhinoceros occulted in the shrubbery outside a modern shopping mall.

He strained to hear the voices, but he couldn't understand what they were saying. Then it hit him. That's what was out of place. The voices were not speaking English! Their dialect sounded sort of like the singsong he'd heard on Hawaiian chants, yet not. And there was something else that was different about the voices. He just couldn't pinpoint what it was.

A shiver ran down his spine. *"Robby, Robby,… what are you afraid of?"* His head was talking to him again. *"Ghosts? Boogeymen? Nonsense! Just move your butt out of this tent and check it out. C'mon, Robby, are you a man or a mouse? Mouse!"*

"Sleepy mouse," he muttered to himself as he threw back the cover on his sleeping bag and rolled onto his knees. Crawling out of his shelter, he noticed gaps were opening overhead in the cloud bank, and through them he could see the midnight sky dotted with twinkling stars. Never had he seen such a sky.

The stars seemed almost close enough to touch. Or were they communications satellites? No matter, it was a beautiful sight. Transfixed by the night he stood gazing at the sky, all thoughts of checking out the voices forgotten in the face of this stellar spectacle. The call of an owl brought him back to reality and he cocked an ear for the voices again. The sound floated clear on the night air the way sound travels over water. No. They weren't in the campsite, they came from the direction of the palis, as far as he could tell. Could there be a settlement up there? Impossible! And yet the voices were real enough.

He looked around apprehensively. What had he expected to find out here? Leprechauns? He sheepishly crawled back into his tent. Yet, he couldn't shake the feeling that there was something strange about this place. The air felt as though it were supercharged with energy. He imagined the stones, grass, trees, shrubbery and even the air itself vibrated on a higher frequency.

Robert inhaled deeply and let his breath out slowly. It felt good. He repeated the exercise. The sound of distant laughter tickled his senses. It sounded exhilarating. How could he sleep with so much going on? He remembered the stories he had read about the Hawaiian little people, and tried hard to recall what they were called. Primo had spoken of them. Moki had met one as a boy. He wondered if he would meet one, too. God! That would be almost as exciting as meeting extraterrestrials!

He imagined himself getting close enough to tape record their language on his Walkman and wondered what the look would be on his ex-English teacher's face when he played it for him. Maybe he'd become the center of attention from top anthropologists from all over the world, a media hero! He smiled and closed his eyes, snuggling into his bedroll, as the sound of fresh rainfall fell on the tent. He fell asleep with the distant sound of musical voices on the breeze.

***

8

Morning dawned through a mottled overcast and Robert crawled out of his tent wondering if his experience of the night before was only a dream. The mossy ground was covered with dew and looked velvety to the touch. He walked around in his bare feet and quickly learned that the green velvet was soggy and slippery, as his feet flew out from under him and he went down with a thud. He picked himself up painfully and hobbled back into the tent to pull his socks and boots back on.

Breakfast was a bag of trail mix and a can of soda pop. A big breadfruit tree dangled its pineapple-like fruit across the clearing, and he named the plants, ferns, bamboo, monkey pod and hibiscus among the luxuriant jumble of vegetation. The remainder were a mystery.

This rain forest was everything he ever wanted in a jungle, and more. Happily whistling to himself he packed up his tent and stowed his gear, hoisting the pack onto his back for today's trek. The Band-Aids on his feet helped to cushion the blisters and he hoped the stiffness would work out of his joints after he'd walked a little way.

The trail took him along a pali ridge and the sheer drop to the sea prompted a sharp intake of breath when he rounded a bend and found himself confronted with a view that seemed to stretch out to eternity. He consulted his map. He could see all the way back to Kee Beach and Haena Reefs. It was a breathtaking view and he focused his camera on it, section by section, cursing himself again for not having thought to buy a wide angle lens.

Moving forward along the lush trail, he imagined he could hear tree sprites calling to him in this enchanted setting. "Rob. Robbeeeee! Come closer. We have many secrets to tell you. Closer, Rob. Listen..." He tilted his head. Of course it was his imagination.

"Robbeeeee... do you see the big rock covered with fungus to your left? I live in here," rumbled the voice of a stone gnome. *"Move closer, don't be afraid, I won't bite."* Robert looked around uncertainly. *"Hey, Kid! I said haul ass over here! Now move it!"* Robert reluctantly moved closer to the rock. *"Good! Do you see the branch laying across me? Be a good kid and move it off to one side, will you? It's blocking my view."*

Robert shook his head and replied aloud. "I guess it must be the altitude, but some weird stuff is going down up here." Nevertheless he moved the branch off the boulder. As he returned to the trail, he could have sworn he heard an audible sigh of relief.

The sun was high in the sky and just past its zenith when he happened upon a waterfall which cascaded into a wide pool at the base of a cliff. The sapphire sky was reflected in the rippling pool and the sun reflected all gold and peach through the mists. If our eyes are the mirrors of our souls, then this pool is mirroring the Earth's soul and reflecting all her beauty, he said silently to no one in particular as the camera lens was focused once again. He'd never been particularly poetic before, but this area was getting to him.

Then he noticed the wild orchids growing around the pool. Quickly, he stripped to his skin and dove into the inviting ripples. He gasped at the surprising cold of the water, at first, which rapidly became tolerable and then pleasant as he swam in the silken liquid. Refreshed and energized from his swim, he climbed up onto a ledge under the waterfall and let the torrent cascade over him, wishing he'd remembered to pull a bar of soap from his backpack first.

Then the magical voices began again. Through the cascading sounds of the water he heard the water sprites singing their greeting. *"How nice of you to drop in,"* they chorused. *"Watch your footing Rob, it's slippery."* *"He doesn't think we're real,"* said one tinkling voice to her sisters. *"He thinks he's imagining things!"*

The sound of crystal laughter followed. *"We'll show you who's real!"* they sang and suddenly the quietly undulating pool of water became a boiling, frothing frenzy as though splashed by a hundred hands. The water rose to his waist and splashed his face, then just as suddenly fell silent again. *"There! You see, Flabby? Do you still think you have an overactive imagination?"*

"He still looks doubtful. Let's give him another demonstration!" The curtain of water abruptly stopped flowing down the mountain and into the pool. Not a drop. He looked up the ridge. There was no water to be seen anywhere, save the pool he was standing in.

The tinkling laughter came again and abruptly the waterfall returned with a thundering roar. He came to life and waded out of the pool as fast as he could. It was uncanny. His skin crawled as the impact of his experience gave him gooseflesh.

The sprites laughed delightedly. *"See Robbeeeee? How can you doubt us now?"*

"I guess I can't doubt you, even if I can't see you," he whispered, as he sat on the bank and dried himself in the sunshine. "But take it easy, hey? A guy can stand just so many miracles in one day!"

The pool glistened like a bath of liquid sunlight. And as he contemplated the beauty of the orchids and the waterfall from his resting place, the voices began to sing to him once again. *"Robbeeeee,"* they chorused. *"We know what's in your mind. We know that you seek adventure and enlightenment. You are so young and your path through life stretches long before you, as it does through the palis, which rim this coast. But fear not. We are with you in the water and our brothers and sisters are with you on the land."*

The voices fell silent. The voice in his head nagged him. Talk back! Reply, dammit! Where are your manners? Yeah, he thought in reply. This may be a fantasy, but why fight it? If I'm crazy, I won't be any less crazy for refusing to talk back. He looked around. "Hello? Are you still there?"

"Yes, Robbeeeee, we were waiting for your thoughts to calm themselves and stop crowding us out. We were saying that we will always be with you, anywhere you go on this Earth. All you must do is allow yourself to grow quiet and listen, and you will never want for our company. We will teach you our secrets' too, and advise you in wisdoms far beyond the understanding of ordinary mortal men."

"That sounds wonderful," he murmured, still feeling foolish at talking to no one in particular. What if someone should see him, reclining on his elbows on a grassy bank, stark raving naked, talking to thin air! He blinked and tried hard to focus his thoughts. If this was reality, it was a kind of reality he had never known.

They read his mind again.

"Come on, Rob. Be flexible! Don't shut us out. Learn to control the noisy chatter in your mind."

He had no idea what to do or say. He felt manipulated by these voices and unsure of himself. And he definitely didn't want to disappoint the water sprites, after the lengths they had gone to, to demonstrate their existence. On impulse, he rose and entered the pool again. Crouching, he cupped his hands and let the cool green liquid filter through. Then the water bubbled and danced around him and he knew it was the sprites playing again.

They were obviously very friendly and he was slowly getting more used to dealing with invisible entities.

"Robbeeeee, you are doing well," sang a high voice. *"We are happy!"*

The current gently caressed his hands and feet. He rose from his crouch and followed his interior voice which urged him to pursue this thing. He cleared his throat, "I can feel you all around me, but it is hard to fully believe when I cannot perceive you with all my senses," he continued. "If my eyes could see you, it would be easier. I don't know your ways, but I am willing to learn if you will be patient with me."

The water bubbled around him in happy excitement. It flashed through his mind that Ral, Larry, Tessa and Vickie would figure he was certifiably schizoid if they could dig him now. The thought made him chuckle. Not that he valued his friends' companionship any less, but this was something entirely different. It felt good. He was communicating with Nature herself; this life was simple and unsophisticated, untouched by the machinations of society. He was sure lucky to have found this place. The water bounced and bubbled around his legs and feet.

"We can see into your heart, Robbeeeee. We know that you are good. And we welcome you to our family. Whenever you have need, just close your eyes and call on us and we'll be there."

"But how will I know? I can't see you, or touch you."

"Yes you can Robbeeeee. We are rain on your face, dew on the grass, ice crystals on your window and fog on a winter night. Our faces are many. We have many ways to manifest..." the voices drifted away.

He stood once more in water that was clear, wondering again if it was his imagination, as he clambered up the slippery bank. He looked at his watch. It was mid-afternoon! How had time slipped away from him like this? There were only about three hours of daylight left. Guess I got carried away, he said to himself. *"So what?"* retorted his inner voice. *"Isn't it all part of the adventure? Why don't you go easy on yourself? Cut some slack. What's your hurry, anyway?"*

"Oh, butt out!" He snapped back. His inner voice fell silent as he pulled on his clothes and boots and hoisted his pack back on. Calling goodbye to the water sprites, he headed back on to the trail.

***

9

He hiked along for two hours, munching on a couple of trail bars as he took his time ascending the winding upward trail. Sunlight slanted through the rain forest and spilled ahead of him in little golden patches which he found himself pacing his stride to step in. Again he congratulated himself on having been fearless enough and smart enough to accept the spontaneous rerouting suggested by Primo. It seemed as though months had passed since he'd ridden through the concrete tourist jungle of Waikiki.

He loved it here on Kauai. He felt as though he were the last survivor on Earth. Then his inner voice returned to remind him it was time to pitch camp for the night. He found the perfect spot. It was on a natural terrace, elevated several feet above the trail and ending in a shallow sort of cutout that would protect him from the rain. His Guide said it rained often up here.

Setting up the tent took only a few moments and soon his kettle was boiling merrily on the camp stove. He fixed a big cup of instant soup and sat just inside the door flap, on his sleeping bag, wiggling his bare toes and feeling like the king of the world.

Finishing his soup, Robert fished in his pack for a beef jerky and his Walkman, munching away as he listened to his favorite tape by Sade. He thought about the events of that day and decided to write them in his journal as soon as he finished his jerky. It was only his second day and already he felt like a weathered world traveler and veteran of the trails. He finished his jerky and pulled out his journal and pen, bending his head to write by the last rays of light as the sun set.

As day turned into night, he scribbled furiously, looking up now and then to monitor the changing horizon which turned from gold to green and pink before finally flooding the sea with crimson until it turned to dusk. What a place! He put his journal and his Walkman away and crawled into his sleeping bag, zipping it up and falling instantly into a delicious sleep filled with beautiful naked wraiths dancing and playing in a tropical pool.

In the middle of the night he was awakened again. This time there was no doubt what had disturbed his dreams. Drums were talking back and forth across the palis, accompanied by happy laughter. Whoever they are out there, they are pretty inconsiderate to travelers, making all that noise in the dead of night, he grumbled.

He turned over and covered his head with the sleeping bag, trying to shut out the noise. It was impossible. He lay there trying to blank out his thoughts, but sleep wouldn't come. The voices were closer than last night. In fact, they sounded very near, as if just around the corner. Maybe I should investigate, he thought, propping up on one elbow.

Investigate what? Don't waste your time, Rob, it's just a couple of locals high on pakalolo, having a private luau. Don't look for trouble. Yeah, he thought. That must be it. I'll just listen to my iPod until I get sleepy again. He didn't want to light his lantern again.

Who knows if those rowdies are near enough to see my light and come snooping around to make trouble? It took a long time of fumbling around in pitch blackness to locate his iPod. Finally he got his favorite music list, and got himself zipped into the bedroll again.

Plumping the sleeping bag into a makeshift pillow under his head, he put on his earphones and punched play. He was in luck, he'd unknowingly selected his ninety-minute collection of mellow ballads by Sade. It wasn't long before he drifted off to the strains of Sweetest Taboo.

PART TWO:
THE ENCOUNTER

10

Robert had not been asleep very long when a clatter just outside his tent awoke him with a start. The first thing that came to mind was bears or raccoons. Whatever was out there was knocking his cooking gear around. Quickly his alarm was replaced by anger. Without his camp stove and pots, how would he cook his food? Reaching for his jeans, he pulled them on and groped for his flashlight and hunting knife.

Psyching himself up for a possibly dangerous confrontation, he pulled on a T-shirt and wished he hadn't left his boots to air out behind the tent. Unzipping his tent flap, Robert emerged cautiously on bare feet as silently as he could manage, flashlight in his left hand, hunting knife poised for defense in his right. There it was, an animal crouched in the roots of a big sea pine. He aimed his flashlight and flipped the switch. Instantly the area was flooded with light.

It was hard to say who was more surprised, the miniature person sitting between the tree roots, or Robert, who had fully expected to defend himself against something with fangs and claws. It was a male, naked except for a loin cloth around his hips. His bare feet were wide and flat, his face was ugly and his belly protruded from a chunky body. A wild bush of matted black hair adorned his abnormally large head.

A while from his chin sprouted an equally wild-looking beard. Transfixed in the glare of the flashlight, his eyes gave off fiery little red glints like those of a wild animal. While Robert wondered what to do, the little guy stood up and crossed his arms over his hairless chest. The look on his face was one of warlike challenge.

Robert stifled a sudden urge to laugh at the comic ferocity of this small, naked, defenseless being who stood trapped in his flashlight beam. This could be one of those little people old Moki had referred to, Menehune! The name came back to him in a spontaneous flash of memory.

Lowering the flashlight so that the beam illuminated the grassy clearing and allowed the little man to see him too, he broke the silence. "Hello there! Welcome to my campsite." He tossed the knife backwards into his tent to show that his welcome was sincere. The Menehune I, you have kaukau? He laughed unexpectedly at this gesture and spoke. His voice was deep and raspy. He made chewing motions with his mouth.

Although the words were foreign to Robert, their meaning was clear. The little guy wanted something to eat. "Aha! So that's why you were rummaging in my cooking gear!" Robert let out a sigh of relief. He held his hand up in a sign to the man to wait, and reached in his tent to extract a can of beef stew from his pack. Quickly, he set up the propane stove, lit it, and waggled the can at the little man to indicate he was going to cook it for him.

The Menehune carefully watched his every move. Then he spoke. "No heat food. Eat cold." "Oh," Robert was confused for a moment. Then he got an idea and rummaged in his knapsack for a length of beef jerky. Unwrapping it, he lay the meat on the paper and handed it to his visitor.

As the Menehune sniffed the stick of jerky and then began to suck and chew on it, Robert had a chance to observe him at leisure. He sure wasn't a pretty sight, but there was pride and dignity in the way he held himself. He carried himself with the bearing of a man who was accustomed to giving orders. Perhaps he was a leader of sorts. Robert was surprised that he felt respectful toward this tiny, aboriginal man.

Finishing his snack, the man handed back the empty wrapper ceremoniously and stood with legs spread and arms once again over his chest. "Alopaka," he said, pointing at himself. "Rob," Robert replied, doing the same. Alopaka repeated the strange name to himself several times as if committing it to memory. "Why... here?" the man asked. "Dis my place."

State park or not, the man apparently thought he had the right to question Robert's presence in the area. "I come as a friend," he was quick to reply. Sounded like a cliché line out of art old TV Western. Good grief, you can do better than that! "I came here seeking peace and quiet. To look into myself. To rest." Alopaka nodded his big head gravely as if understanding the statement and replied. "Many come. Many go. Some stay. You stay?" Then he added an afterthought. "Spirits tell me. You are good."

Robert blinked in disbelief. "Has he talked with the water sprites?" he wondered incredulously. "Why not?" prompted his inner voice. After all, he lives in this jungle wonderland, doesn't he? If you keep on with this kind of thinking, no one will ever accuse you of having an open mind, my boy! Alopaka seemed to sense his inner struggle and nodded his bushy head in agreement.

"Yes. Yes! You listen to little voice in head. He always know." Robert looked at Alopaka, astounded, as his jaw dropped open unconsciously. How can this dwarf read my thoughts? He was annoyed that this Menehune could apparently read him like an open book. Could he have no secrets? No privacy? Hell, I feel invaded! Alopaka watched him placidly, apparently undisturbed by whatever he could read of Robert's inner torment.

"Why you so angry?" he asked at last. "My people listen ant hear da heart speak. Listen with dis," he touched his chest, "not wit' die," he touched his head. "You can learn to listen wit' heart, if you have desire." He poked a finger at Robert. "Simple. Listen to what people think not what people say. You can do."

Robert instinctively knew this was a rare opportunity to explore and maybe learn an aboriginal gift possessed by this Menehune. He did not delay his reply. "Will you teach me?" he asked almost timidly. Alopaka looked at him with eyes full of doubt. "You will do what I say?" he asked.

As he spoke the question his eyes went empty as though he were searching inward for the answer. After a few moments a devilish flicker of light came back into his eyes. "You sure you want to learn?" "Yes. I'm sure." "Wen you listen wat people think, not wat dey speak, you not like dem maybe. Not like dem no mo'."

He would recall this warning two days after his rectum to California, as he interacted with his old friends and family. But at this moment, under a humid Kauaiian moon, he was thirsty for adventure and nothing was impossible. He pushed any lingering hesitation aside, "I want to learn," he repeated stubbornly.

"So, you no mo' happy with yo' old life?" Alopaka insisted again.

"Maybe the dwarf is right? Whispered his inner voice. "Maybe you should say goodbye and get the hell out of this enchanted forest in the morning!" But he knew this was an important choice. And he wanted to carry something valuable away with him when he left Hawaii. He wanted to learn from this aboriginal creature, if he could.

Feeling, as he did, torn apart by the choices confronting him in the fall; poised, as he was, on the threshold of his future and confused, as he felt, over who he really was and what he should do with his life, how could he turn down this chance? His mind was made up. "Alopaka, teach me, Please!" he said firmly.

The dwarf looked up into Robert's eyes and it seemed that there was a trace of pity in his gaze. Why pity? He figured he was imagining things again. "I will teach you." Alopaka replied at last. "Tomorrow we start. Nowh I mus', go." He tossed back his bushy mane of hair and looked up at the night sky. Robert responded to a flash of inspiration and dug in his pack for a cello-wrapped packet of crackers.

"Here, Alopaka, these are for you," he said as he moved forward and placed the packet in his hand. "Spirits spoke truth. You good man." He turned and moved forward quickly into the darkness. "Alopaka, wait! Where will I meet you tomorrow?" Robert called into the darkness. No reply came. I guess he will find me when he wants to, he muttered. Wow! What a story I have for my journal! But who will believe it?

They'll say good old Rob went off the deep end! If I show it to my parents, they'll send me to the shrink. "Robby, you got too much of that Hawaiian sun," he could hear Tessa tease. "Or else he threw some hallucinogenic mushrooms into his stew," her friend Vickie would rationalize with a mock look of concern. Lord only knows what Larry would say, but Ral would be patient and understanding, because that's how he was.

Robert pinched himself painfully on the forearm to make absolutely certain he wasn't dreaming. He was awake, all right! The clear night air felt as though it were charged with energy. He could almost see the energy particles vibrating and pulsating all around him. The air was alive. He inhaled deeply. "It will soon be dawn," he thought. "Better grab some zzzzz while I can."

He returned to his tent and lit his lantern, making notations in his journal while everything was still fresh in his mind. Before he could finish his eyelids filled with lead and he gave in to the irresistible urge to let them close. He turned the key and doused his lantern just in time, before sleep overtook him, and he snored through the dreamless night.

***

11

It was high noon when he stumbled groggily from his shelter, and the sun blazed down relentlessly while he filled a pot with water from a nearby spring and put it on the stove to boil. Armed with a good strong cup of Sanka, he sat on the same sea pine root where the Menehune had been the night before and stretched and yawned.

His muscles ached, his head throbbed. His mouth tasted as though the Russian cavalry had camped there for the night. It felt like a hangover. He mixed himself another cup of coffee and bit into a piece of beef jerky, as dragonflies buzzed around the clearing and put on a display of superb aerodynamics for his sole benefit.

Forgetting his discomfort, he chewed on his brunch and enjoyed the performance. After finishing his food, Robert folded his tent and stored all his gear. He couldn't help but wonder if he should remain here in the clearing and wait for Alopaka to return for him, or continue to hike up the trail and make camp at a more remote elevation. No matter where you go, Alopaka will find you, whispered his inner voice.

Well, in that case, he thought, I would rather find a more remote campsite; one less likely to be invaded by local punks and nudists. "Wouldn't it be a bummer if some insane tourists blundered on the scene just as the dwarf is about to reveal some ancient mystery to me?!" He carried his oversized backpack with ease, despite its awkward bulk, thanks to his football player's shoulders and strong, healthy muscles.

As he started off, his thoughts wandered back to Alopaka and his secret wisdoms. He hoped the little man would teach him to read other peoples, minds. What a trip that would be when he talked with his friends!

Consulting his Guide, he noted a number of ideal, isolated campsites at higher elevations off the main trail above the Honakoa Valley stream. He hurried along the trail at a fast clip, knowing full well he had only four hours of daylight left. As he walked, Robert kept his eyes on the trail, careful not to trip over treacherous lava outcroppings or rogue tree roots.

The only sound he could hear was his own heavy breathing as he progressed steadily upward. The sound of his respiration was hypnotic and gradually his mind left his eyes on watch and turned to thoughts of the Menehune again. He could hardly contain his excitement over the anticipation of his next encounter with Alopaka. He recalled how easily the little man had read his thoughts. He had never encountered anybody with such powers. He had read about it, of course, prophets, gurus, magicians and psychics were supposed to have this talent, but he never really believed it was possible.

What he read and what he believed were very different things. The legends Moki had told him about the Menehunes hadn't included any mention of telepathy. He realized that the Mu people feared contact with the Menehunes for other reasons, and Moki had assured him the Menehunes avoided contact with all other races of people and that they were a secretive and unsociable race. But now he had his doubts over Moki's opinions. Alopaka had seemed friendly enough last night.

His footing slipped suddenly on the mossy stones and before he could recover his balance, he was over the edge and falling at a terrifying speed, bumping and sliding down an almost vertical lava wall. He tumbled, arms and legs flailing, trying to stop himself with his hands or feet, to no avail. His backpack weighed him down, distorting his balance, dragging him mercilessly downward to his doom.

Kicking out with his legs and trying desperately to grab for a passing branch as he tell, he cut his left hand on a thorny piece of scrub pine and felt the skin tear from the palm. "Rob, save yourself," urged his inner voice. There is a jagged lava ridge down there and if you don't stop yourself you'll be impaled!

His left hand was raw and bleeding from the encounter with the bush, but his fall had been slowed. It was then that he fell into a chasm in the lava wall. The wall was angled so that within seconds he was falling through deep shadow. He felt as though the mountain was swallowing him. He wondered if this was an old lava corridor, and his body tensed in anticipation of a bone-crushing impact when he hit bottom. Then it came. He felt a blinding flash of pain and nothing more.

***

12

Robert awoke in the dark with a loud ringing in his ears and automatically reached out to turn off his alarm clock. His hand connected with clammy rock. Then memory flooded back. He had no idea how long he lain there unconscious. He thought of consulting the date readout on his watch, but the thought went unattended because a splitting headache dominated his conscious realm. He shivered, and felt the hair rise on his back in alarm. It was dark and damp and cold in here. He shifted position.

All his bones seemed to be intact, with no small thanks to his backpack still securely strapped around his chest, which must have cushioned his impact, although he could feel the sting of cuts and bruises swelling up. "What now?" he wondered. "I've fallen into the heart of volcanic mountain with no hope of rescue". He unpeeled the Velcro fastener across his chest and struggled to push the straps of the backpack off his shoulders.

His head screamed with pain and his left hand was competing for first place in the agony awards. As he unzipped his pack and groped for his flashlight, that pesky inner voice woke up. "You are one lucky guy there, Robaroo!" it said. "Lucky! You call this lucky? You must be the crazy part of me. Why don't you just shut up?" He lashed back at it, venting his anger and upset at the only person around - - himself. ??? "You could have died in that fall. Your backpack saved you; why not try that idea on for size?" the voice admonished.

That may so, but I still don't consider myself lucky. Lucky would have been catching my balance up on the trail and not falling at all! He continued to feel around in his pack for the elusive flashlight. Where is that damned flashlight? He found it and his heart sank. The glass and bulb were broken. It wouldn't turn on. Then he remembered his lantern. It was made of brass; no way the fall could do more than bang it up. He pulled it from his pack and groped for a pack of matches. There, that's more like it, he said. Now we'll be able to get a little light on the situation.

But the lantern wouldn't light either. He reached back into his pack and pulled out the tee shirt he'd wrapped around the lantern and its smell told him the story. Obviously the battered lamp had leaked out all its fuel. The shirt was reeking of kerosene.

Okay, then, I just need to make a torch, he thought. Using one of his collapsible tent poles, he wound the kerosene-soaked cloth around it tightly tucking the ends into the wind as he had learned to do in the scouts. Then, in the darkness, he couldn't find his box of kitchen matches. Good going, stupid! Fortunately, he remembered the secret cache of matches stored in the head of his hunting knife and laid the torch down while he rummaged in the pack for his knife.

Moments later he had lit the shirt, which was glowing brightly with the kerosene flame. Gingerly, he rose to his knees and held the torch high above his head to see if there was room to stand up. There was more than that. This was a very big cave and the gelling was pitched like a stone cathedral. He couldn't see the top. A few feet from where he'd fallen was the edge of a dark, smooth pool of water.

An underground water table! Must be fed by the fresh mountain springs. He felt a little better, but not much. At least he would have enough food and fresh water to keep him alive for a few days. But who would search for him? Nobody even knew where he was, let alone that he was missing! He wondered if this was night, or if it was this dark in here all the time. Wedging his makeshift torch in a rock crevice, he knelt and cupped his hands to drink from the pool. His left hand screamed out in pain.

Washing it carefully in the dark water, he returned to his pack and pulled out his first-aid kit. A little antibacterial ointment and a gauze bandage wrap, and you'll be good as new, he muttered. While he was at it, he found a headache remedy and used his canteen to wash it down. Refilling the canteen, he set it beside his backpack and looked at his watch. The date was the same, but the time was 11:14 p.m.

He wanted to make his journal entry for the day, but his hand throbbed and his head pounded every time he tried to think. With his good hand, he pulled the torch from its crevice in the wall. There was nothing more he could do for now, and his head was begging him to lay it down somewhere. So, smothering the torch, he reclined against his backpack and mercifully fell into a deep sleep. His last conscious thought was a prayer that the cave would be filled with daylight when he woke up.

***

13

He opened his eyes and registered three sensations simultaneously. His neck was stiff his headache was gone, and there was light in the cave. He looked at his watch. It read 4:00 p.m. He'd slept for nearly fifteen hours! He realized the throbbing in his hand was gone, although it was stiff and tender under the bandage. He took a long drink from his canteen and splashed a little of the water into his good hand and onto his face.

Then he rose to his feet and looked around. There was much more detail to be seen now, thanks to the hazy late afternoon light that seeped in from high above. The pool looked shallow and virginal. He walked around it and saw an opening in the wall about two yards above the water. He wondered if this was a passage that led from this cave to other caves interconnected by the meandering water table.

So intent was he on eyeballing the opening above the pool that he stumbled on something below. Looking down, he saw that it was a huge bone. Perhaps it was a leg bone. It was impossible for him to guess whether it had belonged to a human or animal, but the sight of it made a chill run up and down his spine. "Am I alone in the cave?" he wondered. "Or have I just stumbled on a soup bone from someone – or something's – dinner? Maybe I'm not going to prove so lucky, after all." He hated to admit it, but he was scared. "What now?" asked the inner voice, as if expecting Robert to come up with the perfect solution.

"Any suggestions?" he asked back. "Any idea on how in hell we're going to get out of this mess?" He stumbled on another bone and muttered, oh shit! The urge to leave this place became more imperative. There must be a way out of here. I'll just have to get a grip on myself and calm down so I can explore while there's still enough light to show the detail of these walls.

Around the cave he walked, slowly and carefully examining every crevice and cranny within reach. Nothing led deeper than a foot into the volcanic rock before coming to dead end. He found himself staring at the pool and it's inlet, back in the deepest point of the cave. It seemed to be the only way out. But out to where? Would it lead straight up? Or would it lead into another cave with another pool?

He thought about it. The only way he could explore the inlet of water was to enter the water itself and either wade, or swim. Depending on its depth, back toward the source. He shuddered to think what snakes or other things might lurk in this murky pool. While he considered this next move he stood, surrounded by ominous silence, with only the distant sound of dripping water somewhere in the depths of the cave.

The light was starting to fade now, and he knew there would be no point in attempting further exploration until morning. Well, since I can't go anywhere right now, I might as well cook up some dinner and catch up on my journal before turning in early for the night.

Taking advantage of the remaining light, he turned out his pack and examined all the supplies, reorganizing it systematically. He unrolled his clothing in a little nook in the volcanic rock, not far from his camp, shaking out broken flashlight glass before re-rolling each piece. He found some other tee shirts that were stained with the kerosene and packed them in a plastic zip bag for safekeeping.

If he couldn't get out of here, at least they would provide torchlight for him until they were all burned up. And if he did get out of here, he wound rinse them off in a brook rather than risk fouling his drinking water in the cave pool with kerosene.

Apparently the only casualties of his fall had been

his lantern. "Menos mal!" he exclaimed in Spanish, the elective at which he'd excelled in high school. By the time he'd finished reorganizing his pack, it was very dim in the cave, so he lit his torch and wedged it in the same crevice as before.

He busied himself with lighting the propane stove to boil water for coffee and then reused the pan to cook up a can of spaghetti with meatballs. He was glad he hadn't given all his crackers away to the Menehune. They hit the spot. Then he ate a chocolate bar for dessert and tidied up, being careful to throw his wash-pot water over in a dusty corner of the cave, in order not to pollute his pool.

When he reorganized his pack, he had been able to take stock of the food and calculate how many days' provisions he had left. He figured he could last about five days – maybe seven if he stretched it out – before he was faced with starvation. Starvation. What a meaningless way to die, he grimaced. And he pushed the thought from his mind.

"There must be a way out. I won't give up!" His inner voice didn't protest. It must have been satisfied with his resolve to survive. For a couple of hours he busied himself with a long entry in his journal. "If I don't make it out of here," he wrote, "some day an explorer may find this record and send home news of my fate."

And, despite his resolve to think positive and believe in the eventuality of his escape from this place, he secretly resolved to make a will in his journal tomorrow night, if he was still here. By the time he had written his report, he had a good case of writer's cramp. Gulping down the contents of a warm can of leftover soda pop, he crumpled the empty and placed it in his garbage niche. Then, after setting his wristwatch alarm for seven o'clock, he doused his torch and settled down. Wearing his earphones, he fell asleep while his iPod played an album by Fleetwood Mac.

PART THREE
THE TEACHINGS

14

The wrist alarm went off and awoke him with its insistent intermittent beeps. The moment he opened his eyes he felt a chill. Then he realized he was up to his armpits in water! What's going on? He thought in alarm. Lifting his head from the sodden backpack he stood, ankle-deep in water, and looked around.

The cave was illuminated by the first pale rays of morning light, and the floor was nearly completely covered with water. Worse, he had the sinking feeling that the water level was rising. "Holy smoke! When I was worrying about starving to death, I never dreamed I might have drowned in my sleep instead."

The water was gradually creeping up to his calves and his mind was racing. There wasn't much time. This called for some fast thinking. Robert stood there and scratched his head. He had a strong feeling he had forgotten something important. Something essential. He tried to push down the feeling of panic and remember it. Nothing came, although it was there, nagging at the back of his mind. The water had risen to his knees.

He had to act quickly. He ignored the sinking backpack, waded around to the other side of the pond and tried to climb into the hole in the wall. No luck, he slipped back each time he jumped for it. Suddenly Robert heard a loud splashing sound that was out of place in this silent cave. He looked around in surprise as he spied a big head surfacing near him, shaking the water out of its wooly black mane.

"Alopaka!" he exclaimed with joy. The Menehune moved quickly to his side. "Trouble you got, Rob." he stated with stoic calm. "That much is obvious isn't it?" Rob thought impatiently. But then he turned to Alopaka with a look of benign innocence, "Have I?"

The Menehune caught the look, and laughed. He'd forgotten the little guy could read his mind with ease. Obviously he would know that Robert was scared out of his mind. "Nice of you to drop by," he added. The Menehune ignored this last remark. "Move from dis cave we must," he said. "Filled it will be to level of high puka in wall. Big rain bring much water."

Robert looked down at the rising water, which had reached his hips, and said nothing. "You can swim?" It was half question, half command. The thought of swimming in this mysterious pool was not inviting. "If you want to swim, we'll swim." Robert replied.

Alopaka motioned for Robert to follow and waded deeper into the dark water. When the water reached to his chest, he struck out for the back of the cave, swimming with powerful strokes.

Robert followed on foot, wading in water at waist-level which didn't seem to be getting any deeper, although it was developing a strong current and its bottom was slippery. Stronger and stronger became the current, and Robert fought against it as it pushed him back. "Help dey could," said Alopaka, treading water. "Who?" asked Robert.

Da watah sprites. Why no ask dem? Dey await you call!" Robert fought off incredulity and realized this is what had been nudging at his memory. He shrugged his shoulders questioningly, and silently asked, "How do I call a water sprite?

Alopaka poked him and pointed ahead. They had arrived at a tunnel no more than three feet around. It was almost completely filled with water. Obviously the only way they could get through it would be to swim underwater. "Let's hope you get out of this one alive!" admonished his inner voice. "But how on earth are you going to see where you're going in that blackness?"

Robert closed his eyes and filled his lungs with air. Then he dived after the Menehune swimming blindly into the tunnel. He swam as quickly as he could, hoping he was going in a straight line. He wished there was some visibility in this place, something to navigate by. But there was nothing. He had no idea where Alopaka was either.

Then his lungs signaled that they needed to be refilled. He pressed on. The signal turned into a feeling that his chest would burst. He would suffocate if he didn't get a mouthful of fresh air very soon! He swam on, and it felt as if his heart would explode with the effort.

***

15

Robert panicked and let out his breath, gasping reflexively and drawing in a mouthful of the plankton soup that surrounded him. It tasted horrible! In that second he felt someone yanking him by the hair. His head came up out of the water as he gasped and sputtered and gagged, trying to catch his breath and cough out the vile liquid all at the same time. He could feel a pulse beating wildly in his neck, and he pushed his sticky hair out of his eyes and looked around.

Alopaka stood before him, his arms crossed in their favorite position across his chest as he observed Robert with an odd expression. "You okay?" he asked. "Do I look okay?" Robert replied. "Your hair is a mess." "You are all ovah mess," Alopaka laughed and slapped him on the arm.

"Well, that's encouraging." Robert joked, looking around to see where they were. It was another cave, smaller than the first and apparently slightly more elevated that the one they'd just been in. Although they were standing in a pool of green muck, it was obviously shallow and draining into the one below, since most of the floor was free of water. A weak stream of daylight filtered down from above and he was grateful to be alive and well.

Wading ashore, they sat down to rest. Robert envied Alopaka's simple loincloth. His own heavy clothing was clinging soggily to his body and causing him much discomfort. He began to shiver within the clothing's clamp embrace. "Take off clothing," the Menehune advised. "You be mo' warm. An' dry yo' tings on lava." Robert knew he was right. He removed his bush jacket, T-shirt, boots, shorts and briefs in jig time, laying his clothes out on the rocks to dry. Soon, his skin warmed up and he began to feel better, combing his hair with his fingers as it dried.

He wondered what he was going to do now. He had lost all his belongings when his backpack sank out of sight in the neighboring cave. *Just be glad you did not go under with your gear!*" hissed his unsympathetic inner voice.

"You wanted to eat? But all my food and supplies are gone!" he argued with himself. *"So what, city slicker. Now the real game of survival will begin, pal. You wanted jungle adventure, remember?"* "Yeah, I asked for adventure, not hardship! He snapped. *"Well, Robby, look at your new friend, the Menehune. What does he eat? He sure doesn't look like he's starving!"*

Indeed, Alopaka looked anything but underfed. That was reassuring. New hope dawned in Robert's soul. Alopaka had been observing the young man watchfully. He had read the inner struggle. "Dean is plenty fruits, plenty fish, taro... all you want. No need worry, like me you survive," he said comfortingly. "Rob, you still want me teach you?" He added.

Robert sensed Alopaka's indecision. "Yes, yes. I want to learn." "Yo' life change. Mo' change dan you b'lieve," he warned, absently scratching his matted head. "So what?" Robert laughed. "Some changes would be welcome, Alopaka, believe me!" "You sure?" "Yes. I'm sure. I want to learn. More than ever." Robert stated with as much finality as he could pump into his voice.

He didn't feel very credible, sitting there in his birthday suit. "O.K. Believe I you. And believe you dis, first lesson you just had." Robert waited for the Menehune to continue, to explain, but only silence followed. "What? What lesson?" he asked.

"Lesson of limitations. Five senses limit self. Lesson is learning develop odder senses fo' survive." He formed his sentences carefully and spoke with great concentration.

Robert had the impression that Alopaka was picking up the correct words from out of his own mind. His English didn't seem quite so labored as it had before, although the accent was still strange. Robert marveled at the Menehune's amazing ability to learn. "How do I develop my other senses?" Robert asked.

"Easy. Strain not eyes to see. Strain not ears to hear. Project feelings out from self. What is aroun' you, try to feel. Feel here!" He poked my heart with a stubby finger. "Here is da house of feelings. Close eyes an, reach out. Feel aroun' outside self," he instructed.

Robert closed his eyes. "Good. Now lak' I tell, you do. What sense you wiz eyes closed?"

At first he felt nothing. Then, slowly he began to get the knack of it and it was a great feeling. Simply fantastic! He knew everything that was out there in the cave, without visually seeing it. Then excitement clouded his focus and he opened his eyes with a look of disappointment on his face.

"Stay calm. Sharper is vision won calm," Alopaka

advised. Robert restrained the urge to hug the little man, in case his host had problems with physical shows of affection between males. After all, he had no clothes on.

"Every day you dis will do. Soon you good will be. Soon walk you will across jungle wit closed eyes." Alopaka seemed so friendly and relaxed, Robert decided to venture a question or two.

"Tell me about your people," he began, propping his back against the stone wall for comfort.

"On this island, Menehune many ages ago come." He stroked his beard absently with his fingers. "Befo' brown races come in long canoe, befo' white races come in giant canoe, Menehune race thrive on Kauai." Robert nodded, eager to learn more, afraid to interrupt. "My grandfaddah pass story down, say won first strangers touch our land wit' canoes, Menehune stop live by day ant den live by night. We small peoples, ant first Hawaiian people try turn us into slaves. Menehune no like. We hide. Only at night we work an' play."

"Wait a minute, Alopaka." He couldn't restrain himself any longer. This whole story was beginning to sound bogus. "It just hit me that the first Polynesian settlers migrated to Hawaii hundreds of years ago. How could your grandfather take part in this historical moment?"

"Take part in history because Menehune very long time live. Many hundred years live. Not grow old, fast die like odder races."

"Go on, Alopaka, you're pulling my leg"

"Alopaka tell only truth. How old you think Alopaka?" He asked with a twinkle of merriment in his eyes. Robert looked him over. He could see no wrinkles or other signs of advanced age. "Forty, maybe forty-five at most I'd say." The Menehune laughed heartily. Robert wondered what he had said that was so funny. Or was the little man having a laugh at his expense? But the laughter was contagious and Robert found himself joining in, despite the fact that he didn't know what he was laughing at.

Alopaka wiped the tears of laughter from his eyes. "I am more dan two century old by yo' calendar. Menehune aging not like you, haoles, live long time." Menehune no think age important and all Menehune people know the secret. Use Mana to extend life.

"What is Mana? Something you eat?" Robert was expecting to learn of an elixir that gave them a fountain of youth effect.

"Not eat. Mana is life force. Here in north island, from Hanalei past Na Pali to Kalaulau' Mana is strong. On dis island Mana alive is. In odder places Mana sleeps."

"I've never heard of this Mana before," blurted Robert.

"Mana is channeled from deep in heart of Earth. Go far out to stars. Observe you how stars shine bright, feel close over Na Pali. Dis is effect of Mana."

"Could I use the power of Mana to extend my life span?"

"Yes. Same for everyone. Here, special way to make Mana work for d'em," he explained. "Menehune can teach anyone."

"Then why don't people come from all over the world, the way they do to receive training from the gurus? Everyone wants to have a longer, more productive life span, don't they?"

"People not know. Some know' not believe."

"Yeah, I can see your point. Your race has hidden out here for so many centuries that your first task would be to convince anthropologists that you even exist. Then they would arrive to study your tribe and its mystical religious practices, disrupting everything with their intrusions like they have in their study of other primitives."

"Mo' bettah keep you quiet, Rob. Speak not to others about Na Pali. We no like." Menehune secret people, no like visitors.

"You're probably right, Alopaka. Go on with the stuff about Mana, I want to learn."

"Mana, life force is. Your mind da key is. Flow it will wheah you direct. Training you must have. Discipline you must learn. I will you teach!" his voice held an unexpected note of enthusiasm. "But rest you now. Sun is strong outside. Menehune by day sleeps. Robert by day too must sleep. No mo talk." He announced with finality.

Robert suddenly realized how tired the escape, the swim and the long talk had made him. He checked his clothing. Still damp. But the cave was warm and even the rock at his back didn't feel hard. His body felt heavy and his eyes obeyed. Quickly, he drifted off to sleep.

***

16

He awoke sometime later and checked his watch. Good

thing it was waterproof. It was a little after three, and Alopaka was gone. He wouldn't leave me here like this, he thought. He would never just abandon me.

"Correct you are. Abandon you I would not," Alopaka's voice floated down from above.

Relief flooded Robert's features. "How did you get up there?" he yelled. Alopaka's bushy head was outlined against a crack of bright blue sky. This guy was just full of surprises.

"Yourself, you will dress," he called back.

Robert checked out his things. They were dry as a bone. He quickly redressed himself and tied his boots back on. The clothing felt bulky and restrictive after all those hours of nakedness. Funny how nakedness had come to feel natural and the clothing felt unnecessary. He peeled off the bush jacket and tee shirt, leaving only his athletic shirt on. It felt better, but not good enough, He pulled off the boots and socks too.

"Relax you "What...?" now," the Menehune hollered down at him. "Your mind, make go blank. No link," came the reply. Wondering what Alopaka was up to, Robert forced his thoughts to be quiet and let his circuits level off to a quiet hum. Then it happened. When he closed his eyes he was standing in the cave. When he opened them he was standing up with Alopaka, on top of the lava in bright sunlight.

Robert closed his eyes against the brilliance and cupped his hands over them, letting the light in slowly until his vision had made the adjustment. "I here no lak bettah" grumbled his rescuer. "Dizzy so much sun make me. Shelter we must find quickly." Before Robert had a chance to ask about the levitation trick, he found himself being pulled along with Alopaka, through the bushes on a dead run. Thorny branches scratched his arms as they ran through the bramble. He remembered the jacket he had left down in the cave and wished he'd left it on. Oh well, too late now.

They were moving fast, too fast to seek more soft footing for his tender bare feet. It occurred to him that running through the bush in his tender tootsies was absolutely insane! He wished he had the boots back. Scrub brush and prickly hale koa trees cut his flesh as he ran. He prayed they didn't have much farther to go.

Miraculously, his prayer was answered. Alopaka made a sharp turn out of the underbrush and he followed, to find himself in a clearing before a shelter. An enormous banyan tree stretched its branches of thick foliage over the whole clearing and threw the shelter into deep shade. Vines, hanging from the branches gave the impression they would twine around him in embrace. He wondered mildly if the embrace would be friendly or not. Actually, it was a little strange here in the deep shade, and Robert felt gooseflesh on his arms.

Alopaka, on the other hand, was very much at home. The Menehune swept aside a thick curtain of vines and disappeared inside the shelter. Robert stood, uncertain whether to wait or to follow. He waited. Alopaka reemerged shortly, carrying mangos, papayas and a bowl of smoked fish. He saw that the bowl was made from a dried coconut shell. Placing the food on a mat of wide leaves, the little man sat, cross-legged, and prepared to take his repast. He urged Robert to do the same, so Robert made himself comfortable on the grass next to him. "

Is this your usual diet?" he asked. "Just fresh fruit and smoked fish? Don't you eat meat and potatoes?"

"Menehune eat wot is fresh. Destroyed by heat, Mana is." His tone of voice invited no argument.

Health food nuts, heh?" he thought, as he dug in. "Well, I guess I can live with it."

When they had finished all the fruit they lay side-by-side on the grass and listened to the song of the crickets. What a lovely sound! Robert rolled over and folded his hands under his head for support.

"Robert. Can you feel Mana all around you? Trough you it flows, as through all living tings," Alopaka murmured lazily. Robert closed his eyes. "Can I feel it?" He wasn't sure. He tried to sense the energy. At first nothing happened, but then after several minutes he thought he felt something. It was hard to describe, gentle as a breeze and yet somehow grand and powerful. It pulsated like the beating of an invisible heart.

Wow! What a sensation! So this is the stuff everything is made of. The basic compound. The blueprint for living things. Best of all, I'm part of it! I am it! But am not limited by it. He knew he could easily reach out and touch other life forms, if he wished. Knew he could participate in their existence. Knew that after all everything was part of the whole.

Robert experienced a beautiful, euphoric feeling of joy, almost as though he were possessed of the divine. He no longer felt like a mere mortal, at all. Then, slowly, he emerged from his trance as though awakening from a beautiful dream, to see Alopaka lying next to him, unmoving, eyes closed. His hairless chest moved up and down with peaceful regularity. He was asleep. Robert looked up at the canopy of deep green and tried to analyze what had just happened.

"Possibly it was..." Alopaka's unexpected voice startled him into a sitting position. "...night side of nature you saw. Invisible it normally is to us. Roots it gives to every living ting in dis dimension. Deah it is dat spirits live. Dean it is we go wen we leave physical shell to die. Deah it is we rest until is time to pass to higher plane. You understand?" Robert scratched his head.

"I'm, uhh, not sure," he faltered.

"A place it is wer travel is possible from dimension to dimension while still you are living in yo, physical body." "You mean, I travel around wherever I want, like Peter Pan) or Superman, flying through the air, or something." "I know not dis Peter Pan, or Superman. Dey are haole spirits?" "No. They're storybook characters," at Alopaka's confused look, he explained. "Like mythological persons, flying anywhere like a bird. Superman could even fly to other planets or solar systems."

"Idea you get. But speak I not leaving crude physical body on Earth ant in your luminous body traveling to stars, universes, dimensions, like dat" Alopaka paused long enough to let Robert digest this information. "You understand, Rob? Questions you have?"

Questions, yes?! He thought he should start with something simple. "Have you traveled to the stars, Alopaka?" "Traveled to other planets, I have," he affirmed solemnly' then added, "This, even our children can do!"

"No kidding? I'm sorry if I don't seem to be taking this all as seriously as you might like, my friend, but this sounds like a segment from 'That's Incredible'."

"Explain." Alopaka said with a frown.

"It's a television program that shows incredible people and events to people who have never seen anything like it before."

"Television?"

"Oh boy! I'm probably getting you in over your depth. Television is the teleportation of a moving picture which shows up on a box about this big'" he gestured, "with a sort of mirror on it. You look at the mirror and see the picture. We call it TV for short."

"I like see dis mirror box. More evolved than I expected yo' haole civilization must be."

"In a different way from yours, Alopaka. We have some good things in our culture," Rober said. "But tell me, what else can your children do?"

"Anyting dey want, on education from parents dis depends. Dey levitate, can to plants ant animals talk, can mo' faster make plants ant animals grow. Fo' instance. Vaporizing clouds, pastime fo' children is. Compete dey do, fo' who vaporize largest cloud."

Robert watched him with his mouth open. Alopaka looked up selected a fluffy, white cumulus cloud riding high over the treetops and looked back at Robert again.

"You see cloud hanging over mountain peak?" Robert saw it all right. It was big and heavy, moving majestically over the rugged cliffs. "Watch!" commanded the Menehune. Robert looked at the cloud, which did a disappearing act right before his eyes. He stared at the place where it had been for several moments. Now, all he could see was the powder blue sky. He felt that gooseflesh again, licked his dry lips and tried to think of something laid back to say. Nothing came to mind. "Do it you can, if you practice," promised the dwarf, ignoring Robert's confusion and grinning proudly from ear to ear. "Try now."

"Oh, no! I couldn't do that. It's impossible!" He was terrified by Alopaka's reckless demand.

"Start we must with you attitude," the Menehune announced in a firm tone. "Attitude is main problem. Rob, tell me why you cannot?" "I can't do it because... because... because it can't be done!" he stammered, and then realized how stupid that was. Hadn't he just seen it happen?" "It you saw done, yes?"

"Yes, yes. I did. I'm sorry." He was in total confusion.

"Sol. You now do it. Go!" Alopaka demanded pleasantly.

Robert selected a very small white cloud and stared at it intently. Hocus pocus! He commanded in his mind. The cloud continued to float lazily along, unmindful of his directive. I must be doing it wrong. He tried another approach. Projecting his thoughts outward, he tried to chase the little cloud away. This time he closed his eyes while he concentrated. When he opened them, he thought he observed an alteration in its shape and position. Keeping his eyes open, he found he could push the cloud with his thoughts, move it to any place he wanted it to be.

"For second lesson, not bad," congratulated the Menehune. "Simple it is, Rob. In yol mind limitations are, remember dat. In yo' mind limitations you create. Exist dey do not, outside yo' brain. Believe you, and you will achieve. Impossible nothing is!"

"I think I've known this basic fact for some time, Alopaka. I just never acknowledged it before."

"Caution you I must, Rob, to not use power fo' harm. All who use must obey. Always remember." Robert was glad Alopaka was improving his vocabulary through telepathy but the lapses into poor English were comical and his syntax would give old lady Kimball, his grammar school teacher a cardiac arrest.

This guy is something no one will ever believe, he thought bemusedly.

"Courtesy to oddah life forms, spirits and non-human beings you must always show. Depend we do on each oddah in die plane and share we mus' in da balance of all nature. Different tings might be, yet respect we must. Important die is in yo' training," he concluded.

Robert had a flashback to the civilization he had come from. Purveyors of wars, acts of violence, crime, starvation and suffering' with dog-eat-dog and very little, if any, respect for anything, He felt ashamed.

Alopaka had read him again. "Yo' place it is not to worry fo' dem," he said gently. "Evolve dey will, in time. Mistakes we all make an pay for dem we do. Learn from dem we mus', because, b'lieve or no, universal order is perfect. Examine please, dis leaf."

He bent to lift a leaf from the ground. It was a round, green, perfectly shaped leaf from the hau tree.

"Look dis leaf Rob! Shaped it is so perfectly. Like night sky wit stars so perfectly arranged in firmament. Stars all in motion, nevah crash. No chaos, no confusion. According to perfect plan everyting work."

"Makes sense," Robert agreed.

"Den you see? From us all imperfections come.

From us all frustrations born. Within us insecurities reign. Chaos we create. Know you why? Because forget we do who we are. Forget we our heritage as glorious beings wit limited powers." He smiled and picked up the coconut dish again. "Now. One mo' smoke fish let us share' I hungry again!"

Robert blinked in surprise at the abrupt change of subject. "This Menehune guide of mine sure manages to keep me off balance!" he mused, helping himself to another piece of smoked fish. As they chewed in silence, Robert struggled to digest all the information Alopaka had vested in him. Somehow, much of what he'd had to say was not foreign to him. In some way it was more like he was reawakening to a knowledge he'd possessed from the beginning of time.

***

17

After eating, they rested on the grass. Alopaka fell into a deep sleep and snored loudly because he was not accustomed to being awake during the day.

Robert couldn't fall sleep, so he tried to meditate and ended by just letting the afternoon drift by, happy in the realization that he was free from that tomb of a cave and back in the real world again. Towards sundown Alopaka roused himself and got to his feet. "Thoughtful you were, to let me sleep Rob. Show you around I will," he offered.

"Thanks, but it'll be dark, soon. Not much point in you touring me in the dark. How about tomorrow morning... " But Alopaka had set out at a fast clip into the rain forest and Robert had little choice but to follow. After they had traveled some distance, Robert became aware of the fact that he was pursuing his host heedless of his bare feet.

"See, Rob? You can do anything, if you set your mind to it!" his inner voice was needling him, as usual. Big deal, he scoffed back. "Ouch!" he called out, having at that moment stepped on a thorny twig. Limping along, he tried to brush off whatever had caused this pain.

"You O.K.?" His host looked back in concern.

"Not sure." His big toe was sticky with blood and sending little needles of pain into his foci.

"Let me see." Alopaka pulled him down until he sat on a boulder.

Taking the wounded foot in both hands, the Menehune mumbled an incomprehensible phrase under his breath and stroked the foot for a minute. Then, lowering the foot he said, "You are well. We go on now." Robert felt for the Injury with his hand. There was no blood and no sore spot that he could find. He stood. No pain on standing, either.

He turned around to thank Alopaka and saw that his friend had run on ahead, causing him to run after him. The little guy could sure move! Robert only kept pace with great difficulty.

As they ran through the rain forest, the sun sank into the ocean and night fell over Na Pali coast. Soon, the moon rose to fill the scene with an eerie, beautiful silvery light. The rain forest looked like a fairy kingdom. The ghostly vines and trees were shining with drops of dew and looked for all the world as though everything was sprinkled with moondust.

"Where is my Menehune taking me?" he wondered as he ran, climbed and even levitated in places where the terrain was insurmountable on foot. Levitation was beginning to seem like a very normal action, now. He felt as though he had done it all his life.

At last, Robert and Alopaka reached the summit of a mountain, which towered five thousand feet above sea level. It was humid and misty at this altitude and Robert could see clouds floating beneath them like silver cotton floss in the night.

"Home of MU dis is," said Alopaka with a grandiose sweeping gesture at the vast panorama. "Here live MU people," he continued, "in isolation still. Protect demselves dey must from da intrusion of curious humans."

"Well, they sure won't be bothered much at this altitude!" said Robert, trying to catch his breath in the thin air. "With yo, world MU people were da original link. From da cosmos dey came. Remaining are very few full blood MU people, now."

"What happened to reduce their numbers?"

"Ventured into early Hawaiian society, dey did. Killed, some wer. Intermarried, others wer. Also da curtain many others crossed."

"Curtain?"

"Odder side." the dwarf sounded a little cross, as if Robert should know what curtain meant.

"Where? How?" he insisted, intrigued.

"World parallel to dis, you know? Heard you not of Honopu Valley, o' Valley of Lost Tribe? Home dis valley was to dem befo, dey crossed."

"A whole tribe? Into the parallel dimension? Just like that? They must have had some motivation," Robert scoffed unbelievingly. "Come on, Alopaka. You've got to be pulling my leg."

"Leg I no pull. Why you say dat?"

"It's an expression we have when we want to tell someone we're finding them hard to believe."

"Learn you not from my teachings? Know you not dat I always speak truth?" He gazed sadly upon the young man before him... Look dat mountain," he said as he pointed to a neighboring peak shrouded in mist. "Beyond it can you see wot lies? No! Say you then dat wot you cannot see cannot exist? Foolish you! Odder things of life, same. Wit' limited senses of vision, smell, touch, taste, feel we live only in physical realm. For odder use extra senses we have. Beyond we reach, da hidden we find, da odder reality is no less real." He paused reflectively. "But now die moment let us enjoy. Special is dis place. Mana current flows strong where we stand. Like river of energy joining da Earth an' sky. Flow through you it will, if you allow. Relax, Rob and happen it will."

"Yeah? Don't tell me, Alopaka, that you have also been to the other side of the curtain?" asked Robert with unveiled disbelief.

"I have!" the little man fairly bristled.

"Lives there in Valley of Lost Tribe part of my family. Two bruddahs an' many cousins live der." Alopaka mentioned it as if it was the most commonplace thing in the world to have family living in another dimension.

"Can you describe what it is like beyond the

curtain?" Robert was consumed with curiosity.

"Much like here, different also. Odder side of curtain closer to dark side of nature. Never shine bright sun. Never see stars or moon. Sky is hazy, like milk."

"Sounds like Los Angeles."

"Say again?"

"Nothing Alopaka, an inside joke, please go on."

"Odder side beautiful is Robert. More alive is nature deah. Spirits of Nature are everyday part of life deah, like family. Some call da land Misty Island. One day I take you deah, if you want."

This was almost too much for Robert's wondering ears. Did he dare to believe this ugly little man? Would he ever have the nerve to try going into another dimension with him. And if he did, would he ever return, or would they get trapped there? *Whatever happens I'll never be able to tell anybody back home. They'll put me away for sure!* When he came back to the present, he found Alopaka staring at him inscrutably.

"Robert! Where you go? I ask you relax and let Mana flow, but you think about Los Angels people instead."

"Los Angeles, Alopaka, not 'Los Angels'," Robert laughed. "I apologize. I'll clear my mind like you taught me, okay? Here we go."

Robert did as he promised. Yes! The Mana, the life force, was flowing through his veins like an electrical current, prickling his skin. The voltage of high energy excited his nervous system and set his fingers and toes to vibrating so strongly he nearly laughed out loud. Sometimes he wished he weren't so ticklish. He closed his eyes and tried to go with the flow. He tried to be at one with it as he had before. But he was ill prepared for what happened next.

The flow lifted his spirit, swept him off his feet and left his body standing on the mountaintop as he sped off toward the stars. From his lofty perch he looked back at Earth and reached out emotionally to that breathtakingly beautiful blue globe and called out with love in his heart to all his fellow creatures. The reply came back before long. His message was returned by billions of beings from all over the galaxy.

The feeling of unity was so strong that he was nearly overwhelmed. He was one with the very stuff of creation. Happiness welled in his heart and both his exhilaration and depth of feeling reached out with no limit. In the instant of that response he knew with certainly that man was not alone in the Universe. He knew there were millions of life forms on billions of planets, and he felt the joy of a shipwrecked sailor who has discovered civilization again.

Nearly simultaneous with this knowledge, he found himself rapidly descending to the planet's surface once again and home to his body where he belonged, at least for now.

Not speaking, walking as if on air, he followed Alopaka down the mountain to his shelter under the banyan tree. There, on grass mats, they laid down as the first light of dawn streaked the sky. All day, they slept. Robert's dream world was exciting, colorful and kaleidoscopic, as never before in the history of his young life.

***

18

The next night, Alopaka took Robert to see some of the Menehune stone constructions built in the past when the culture was flourishing. He saw fishponds, heiaus, and miles of aqueducts, to name a few. Pointing to a series of high lava-stone walls, Robert said. "What was the purpose of these?" They appeared to have been built for no apparent purpose.

"Built dey wer in times wen daMenehune race still not reach high level of wisdom. Not have understanding of laws of nature. Practice, we did primitive magic at dat time. History of my race dese walls contain. Each stone contain wish an' imprint of mind of ancestor who place it dean." "What kinds of wishes?" "All kinds. Wish fo' good fishing, rain wish, healing wish, birth wish. All kinds. Leaders make wish fo' peace everywhere. Alive are wishes still in da stones after many century. Working to fulfill wish many still are. Amazing' o' what?" "Amazing' yes!" Does this man have any idea how mind-boggling some of this stuff is to my ears?

"Believe you will, in time Rob," Alopaka said, tuned in to his thoughts as usual. He kept forgetting that even his thoughts were public information with this gnome around. Alopaka picked up a loose stone from the top of a small pile and touched it to his forehead, in the exact place where the third eye is supposed to be, just above his eyebrows. He seemed to be listening intently to some unheard message.

"Dis stone was place heah by Lanipo. Leader was Lanipo, he come from place now called Maui. To exchange news he came. To wish fo' peace tween

Menehune people ant yo' people he came. He use die stone to wish fo', peace an, understanding between us, so yo' peoples not capture an' enslave us. Still alive is his wish. Inside da stone it still lives. Hopeful is da wish dat one day da message will be answered in da hearts of all da peoples of da world. Glad day dis will be. Happy day fo' rejoice'" Before Robert could comment, the Menehune had another stone and listened to it as intently as he had the first. "Dis stone belong to young picked up Menehune maiden who fell in love wit` a MU man. Man pass beyond curtain. Girl wish to reunite wit' lover.

Faddah of girl command her stay wit, family on dis side. Heart of young girl is broken an, she make powerful wish. Den lover return fo' her one night ant take her away wit him. Break faddah's heart. But young girl nevah regret wish, altho' miss family fo'eva."

"Hey! That was some story' Alopaka. Have you ever thought of writing a book?"

"Say again?"

"Never mind. Come to think of it, I haven't seen a piece of paper or a pencil since you found me. Guess that's why your people needed talking stones, huh?"

"Yes, Robert. We talk stories, pass da events by song an, story ant wishing stones tell many tales. Each stone have story to tell. You try. Yes! Be not afraid, Robert, pick one!"

Robert gingerly picked up a stone and held it to his forehead as he had seen Alopaka do. He couldn't help but feel a little silly, but there was no turning back with the Menehune's beady eyes fastened upon him. The stone felt cool. He listened. At first all was silent. Then he was startled by a sudden rush of images in his mind.

He heard a whisper, a sort of chant. It must have been in the ancient Hawaiian tongue, but somehow he understood its meaning. The wishing stone held a prayer to quiet the storm that had been raging then. He could see the billowing, angry clouds and see the forest lashed by high winds. A small, chunky figure of a man was sitting by a fire that was nearly out.

He was beating a rhythm on his long drum covered with sharkskin, and the beat was repetitive and monotonous. His wish was very strong and clear; he was asking the spirits of the air to calm the wind. A gust of wind blew the embers of his fire into an explosion of sparks, and as the man put the stone down in order to pour sand over the fire pit, the image faded.

"Hey, that was something else!" he exclaimed. "Not even Steven Spielberg would believe this!"

He saw the look of puzzlement on Alopaka's face and rushed on.

"Hey, that was just like a video tape, with sound track and all!"

"Video tape?" Alopaka repeated uncomprehendingly.

"Oh yeah, you've never seen TV, I guess." I've done it again! He thought. I keep confusing this dude with references to my world that he can't understand. "Well, what I'm saying is I saw a picture and heard the chant and I understood it all. It was fantastic!"

"Ah. Good. You learn quickly my boy." "What now, Alopaka? The night is young and the moon IS full, and I'm wide awake." Robert winked at his friend. "Shall you take me to meet a lovely Menehune maiden?"

"No. Maybe next visit you meet Menehune family.

Dey no trust you yet. Must give time fo' be accepted."
Robert looked so disappointed that Alopaka nearly
relented, but then a new idea occurred to him. "Nevah
mind, young man. I show you mo bettah fun. Come!
Now we go walkin, on da pond." Robert was not a bit
surprised at this sudden change of topic, and mood, he
was getting used to Alopaka's capricious personality.

"Pond walking?"

"Place weah human nevah set foot is Ponokai pond.
Only Menehune go deah. I show you most unusual place
on island. Let's go!' Robert nodded and they plunged
deeper into the rain forest. Mokihana berries were
ripening and gave off a strong anise odor that permeated
the night, a scent Alopaka evidently loved. He stopped
and filled his lungs with it, wearing an expression of
visible enjoyment.

They emerged from the forest onto a moonlit
savannah channeled with narrow ponds lined with
volcanic rock. "Hey, they'd make good lapping pools!"
cried Robert, momentarily forgetting himself.

"Lapping? Explain!" Alopaka stopped and threw
him a funny look.

"Oh, sorry. It means a place where you practice
swimming. Long, narrow lanes of water like you have
here."

"Menehune practice swimming in ocean. Grow fish
in ponds. Come!" He grabbed Robert's hand and pulled
him toward the rock wall lining one pond. "Trust!" he
said.

Robert had no option but to follow. "Wait!" he said.
I will remove my pants and shirt."

Alopaka laughed.

"No need."

"Sorry friend, but I'm going to have to ignore you on this one." There was no way he wanted to get into the water with all his clothes on! He quickly pulled off his pants and athletic shirt, leaving his briefs in place. He could leave them hanging on a bush to dry tomorrow while they slept.

Together they climbed over the retaining wall and into the pond. Strangely enough, his feet didn't slip on mud. In fact the water seemed to give gently under him without letting him sink into it.

"Alopaka, look! I'm walking on top of the water!" He clung tightly to the little man's hand, afraid that if he let go, he would surely sink. He had no idea what lay under the impenetrable black of the water, and he had no inclination to find out.

Alopaka was strolling along as casually as though he were taking a walk across his clearing by the banyan tree. "No come heah my people no mo'," he commented. "Undisturbed for die reason, die area is. Clear tings become to me wan I walk heah. Directly can I learn da answers to problems from da causal plane. Open to me is da night side of nature in dese ponds."

"There is so much for me to learn, and so little time," Robert complained as he was drawn along.

They walked for a while in total silence. Only the water occasionally splashing under their feet disturbed the silence, as a fish jumped from the pond's mysterious depths. While little wisps of fog hovered over the banks where lush vegetation hung down to meet the water.

"Robert, wish you to see anyting or maybe one person from da place you call Los Angels? Or answer to question you can have?"

Robert noticed the Menehune's distortion of his hometown's name again, but let it pass. Perhaps he had the best name for it, anyway. He tried to think of just one thing. One important thing. His mind was overloaded with dozens of questions, all clamoring for an answer, but he wanted to choose something important.

I could ask him what I should do with my life, he thought. Or I could ask to see my mom, or someone. Involuntarily the image of Tessa popped into his mind. Her pretty face and flushed cheeks were laughing gaily at something. I wonder how I could see something so far away? Alopaka had been listening to his thoughts again. "Easy, Robert. Just follow me."

They walked to the exact middle of the pond and the Menehune knelt on the dark surface of the water, which gave under his weight with about the same displacement as if he had knelt on a waterbed. He motioned for Robert to kneel beside him. The silver moon reflected on the water's surface like a shimmering disk. "Now look at da reflection." commanded the dwarf. "Fix yo' mind on dat ting you want see an' you see it will."

Robert knelt beside Alopaka and gazed into the shimmering reflection of the moon on the water. He thought of Tessa, tried to picture her. Nothing happened. This is really silly, he groaned internally. Might as well buy myself a crystal ball, for all this is worth. I just don't have what it takes.

"See you will wot you wish to see. Right, heah? Patience, young man!" Alopaka poked his finger at the surface. A splash resulted and little rings of wavelets radiated outward.

Robert decided to try once again, for his host's sake. He stared long and hard at the water's surface, and the longer he stared the funnier he felt. Finally, he began to feel a little woozy and his vision clouded. Then it cleared and he saw Tessa smiling at him. Her image was as clear as a hologram, it had dimension as though she were there. She spoke but he couldn't hear her words. But he saw her lips move and he thought he saw her say, "I love you, Rob." Then, just as unexpectedly as she had come, she left. Her image wavered and flickered out like the flame to a candle. "Hey, Tessa, don't go!" called Rob.

"Your mind you let wander. Da image cannot stay won replaced by anoddah. Close eyes and tink of replacement, den open again, see who come." He did, and the concerned faces of his mom and dad appeared. They were sitting in the study, discussing him. Robert felt a pang of guilt, and quickly erased the picture. He wasn't ready to go home. They strolled all night on the ponds and arrived at the clearing of the banyan tree just before the first light of dawn. The day was spent a slumber in the deep shade. Robert had adapted to the rhythm of Menehune life without noticing it. And so the days and nights passed in Alopaka's company, with Robert learning of mysteries and wonders beyond his wildest dreams.

***

19

His trusty watch told him it was August 10th. Where had

the weeks gone? It was time to return to civilization, to reality and to his world in Los Angeles. He felt sad. Never in his life had he felt so unwilling to leave a place. A whole new world had opened up for him here on the Na Pali coast, and he agonized between the fantasy of life in the rain forest and the pull of his family and obligations back home.

Alopaka knew full well what the young man was feeling. He taught Robert to dive from the cliffs, a favorite Menehune recreation. They would find a big rock, throw it out into the ocean and dive for it. The coral reefs and shallows made this a dangerous sport for any ordinary folk, but for Alopaka it was no big deal. He would launch himself off the cliff and disappear into the turbulent waters of the reef far below, to appear shaking his wooly head like a dog and holding the stone up for Robert to see.

The first time it was Robert's turn, he looked down at the foaming reef surge and felt weak. A hundred yards of sheer volcanic rock face and boiling surf invited him to his death. If I miscalculate, I'll smash to smithereens on the rocks, heaped at the thought. And the longer he considered his options, the harder it became for him to jump.

"If I miscalculate, I'll smash to smithereens on the rocks." He grew pale at the thought. And the longer he considered his options, the harder it became for him to jump.

"Hey, Rob! No guts?!" his inner voice challenged. He took his position and closing his eyes, prayed to providence for protection. Then he threw his rock out, took a deep breath and dove. After what seemed like an

eternity, he felt the sting of impact as he entered the cool Pacific ocean, and surfaced through a wave. Where is my stone? I've made it this far, wouldn't want to mess up now! He dove into the surf, searching by the bright light of a full moon.

A strong swimmer, Robert was not trained to stay underwater and soon he had to resurface to fill his bursting lungs. Where is that devil rock? Then he spotted it, drifting slowly downward, only a few yards away from him. Kicking rapidly, he made his way to the rock, grabbed it and surfaced without delay. Breaking the surface, he gasped for air. Alopaka sat on a boulder beside the reef, placidly watching the surf crash all around him.

"Good! Robert, good!" he approved, as he helped his disciple up on the rocks. Robert was breathing heavily at the exertion and sat motionless for a long time. What's more, the boulder upon which he sat was very slippery with algae and he feared the slightest move would send him sliding down into that surf again.

After a long silence, Alopaka spoke up. "Sorry I am to see you go away," he said in a low voice.

"I'll be sorry to say goodbye to you, too," he returned, "but I must go back to my people, Alopaka. My responsibility calls to me and it is time to go." Then he was hit by a sudden thought. "Would you like to come back to L.A. with me? I would like to show you my world, too."

"Me? To city? What joke you make," he slapped his thigh and rocked with laughter.

"No joke. Listen, Alopaka, using your knowledge and abilities you could be a rich and powerful man in my society. You could control people and industries. You could command a position of importance!" "Why I want rich? Why I want position? Will position and riches happy make me?" The little man peered closely at Robert's face and he felt as though he were looking right into his soul.

Robert realized the foolishness of his proposition. Of course it was unthinkable for this aboriginal man to visit L.A. What could he have been thinking? Anyway, Alopaka could materialize a city right here in the jungle, if that's what he wanted. He knew the little man had every comfort right here. This jungle was his home. "Yes, everything right here fo' happiness," Alopaka murmured as if echoing Robert's thoughts.

Well, he needs his world and I need my world. We must each live with our own realities, Robert thought.

Alopaka again echoed his theme. "Yes, Rob. Depends on point of view, does reality. Diff'rent reality serve diff'rent people. Yo' reality no wrong reality, just yo's, different not wrong. Accept we must the diff'rences as we embrace da similarlties. Judge no tween mends. All ways are good." Robert nodded solemnly. "Robert, I give you formula fo' make yo' own magic. Remember dis: imagination plus concentration plus willpower will bring manifestation of anything you desire."

"Yes, I know. You've taught me that, and much more."

"Easy, yeah? Easy when da knack of it you get."

"Alopaka, I owe you so much. You have taught me so many wonderful things. I wish there was something I could do for you, too. But I can't think of anything I can do that you can't do for yourself." He laughed. "It's like in the Christmas catalogs I've seen that say for the man who has everything, and then shows a picture of a golden toothpick. Well, you're a man who has everything you want, and I have lost everything I owned. Except my watch. Would you like my watch?" "No watch. Alopaka no need. Have gift already."

"You have? I don't understand."

"Gift you give. Notice you how good I speak English now? Dis is gift you give me, Rob. Dis is good and lasting gift." He looked at Robert intently as though waiting for agreement.

"Oh yes! Your English is really good now. Perfect! I'm proud of you." He reached out and squeezed the Menehune's hand.

"Den gifts we have given each oddah. We good friends." Robert felt the tears well up in his eyes.

He hunched and wrapped his arms around his legs, lost in thoughts of leaving.

PART FOUR
THE RETURN

20

"So! You have met da Menehune!" cried old Moki' opening his cabin door to Robert's knock at dusk, "an' dey have rob you of all yo' possessions! Come in' my boy! Take refuge ant tell me all about it!" He pulled the disheveled, barefoot young man into his kitchen and put a kettle on to boil.

"It's good to see you again, Sir." Robert's reply was truthful. The sight of that kettle promised a nice cup of hot herbal tea and he could hardly wait. The walk down the mountain had taken all day, and although his feet were well calloused by now, he was bone weary and hungry as a bear. Robert flopped into a chair (a chair -- such a luxury!) and closed his eyes while Moki fussed over the stove, reheating some rice and making a quick stir-fry in his wok. Setting the steaming food before the young man, he urged him to eat.

"First mol bettah you eat. Den we talk if you no are too tired."

"Bless you Moki. I don't know what I would have done if you weren't here. I sure am hungry enough to eat a bear!" Moki stood by and watched Robert gobble the food. It was obvious he could hardly contain his impatience. When the plates were empty, Moki handed him a bunch of small ripe bananas and washed up the soiled plates. Then, placing the teapot and cups on the table, he sat.

"Now tell me all. Where you go fo' mo' dan two mons? An' wot happen to dat pretty outfit you wear wen you come heah befo'? Went rob you, ol wot? Da Menehune?"

"No, Moki. I went climbing and fell down the mountain and landed in a big cave. Then the cave started to fill with water and I would have drowned, but a Menehune found me and saved my life. Unfortunately my backpack sank in the water of the cave."

"No kidding? You one lucky fella, dear Robert. A Menehune, he no hurt you o' make bad magic wit' you?"

"No. He showed me Na Pali from mountaintops to the reefs below. He shared his food and told me many stories. He taught me many things. He was a good man, Moki, the best! Good, and generous, like you. I owe him my life and a whole lot more."

"I find dat hard to believe, Son, even tho' I have no reason to doubt wot you say."

"Believe it, Moki. Now, I have some favors to ask of you, if you don't mind. I'll need to get to a phone in order to call my parents on the mainland, and I'll need a place to sleep until they can arrange my airfare home. And I'll need a ride into Lihue whenever I can get a reservation back to L.A. I know it's a lot to ask, but I can repay you whatever you think is fair."

"I link is fair if you stay keep me company one, two days ant den let me drive you Lihue way. I need buy some parts fo' da truck' anyway."

"You're a real friend, Moki. I just hope that old clunker of yours makes it to Lihue in one piece!"

"Yeah, I hope, too!"

Moki laughed and Robert joined in. Driving anywhere in that pile of junk was an experience.

***

21

The next morning, Robert slept late. Then, after a breakfast of eggs and deep, rich coffee, Moki told him to retrace his steps to Tutu's store and there he would find a telephone. It was lucky he reversed the charges when he called his mom because he ended up talking to her for nearly an hour after she recovered from the shock of hearing from him for the first time since he left home.

Having decided not to reveal the true story of his adventure until he had more time to think about it, he shaded the truth and told his mom he had lost his backpack containing all his possessions, and even lost his boots, when a wave knocked his things off a reef rock and drowned them in the sea. It was decided she would send him a money order and return ticket home to L.A. through the airline company. He asked mom to make the reservations for him at her end, and told her he would call the inter-island airline reservation desk tomorrow for confirmation, assuring her that meanwhile he was the guest of the grandfather of a friend.

He spent two quiet days in the company of old Moki, and during that time shared with the old man most of his experiences with the Menehune. He had no trouble being believed. The old man had heard stories better, and worse, in his time.

"Many people have climb da Na Pali," he said. "Some lose da gear, some lose da mind. No stay da same."

***

22

He didn't know whether to feel sad or relieved to be reserved on the Hawaiian Air flight to Honolulu, where he would connect with his United flight back to L.A. Moki let him off outside the passenger check-in area and waited beside his truck while Robert picked up his ticket and had the airline cash his mom's money order. Then they trucked the couple of miles back into Lihue town where Robert hastily bought an aloha shirt, white cotton duck pants and canvas shoes. After taking Moki for a quick lunch at the pizza place, they rattled their way back to the airport.

It was time to say their goodbyes. The old monkey of a man and the strapping young haole hugged each other with great tenderness. Robert pressed a fifty-dollar bill into Moki's hand despite loud protests. "I will write to you, Moki."

"I no write, I nevah go school."

"That's okay, Moki. I'll send you cards at Christmas or whenever I travel to some other place. You can get Tutu to read them to you." The flight to Honolulu took less than half an hour, and with no luggage to transfer, Robert saw that he had an hour and a half to kill before he had to board the flight to L.A.

Killing time was no problem; he had the perfect solution. He sprinted outside to the SIDA taxi area and asked the dispatcher if Primo was on duty that day. The answer was affirmative. All he had to do was sit in the shade of a planter and wait for Primo to report back from driving his latest fare. The jug-eared man pulled in about 10 minutes later and when the dispatcher informed Primo he had a fare waiting, he failed to recognize Robert when he climbed aboard.

"Hi, Primo. Do you remember me?" The quizzical expression told him he did not. "You gave me your granddad's address in Hanalei a couple of months ago, remember?"

"Hey! Howzit Robert! I nevah recognize you with dose long curls and aloha wear."

"Ha! I guess you're right, Primo. I didn't realize how different I must look."

"Where you like go Robert?"

"Let's just go and have a cool drink somewhere, Primo. I've got a little over an hour to kill, and I have news of your grandfather."

"Okay brah. I drive to Kelly's over on Lagoon and Nimitz. Dey have coffee shop an, bakery. I think you like. I take my break now, stay 45 minute, den take you back."

Robert had a pastry (a delicious corruption of civilization) and coffee while Primo wolfed down an order of lemon chicken. They exchanged animated conversation between mouthfuls, and Robert gave Primo enough information on Moki, Tutu's store and the Na Pali hike to satisfy without going into too many details. Then Primo got him back to the airport just in time to board his flight for L.A. Easing into a plush first class window seat on the big 747, Robert was glad his mom had spoiled him this time. He located a channel of mellow Motown on his earphones and accepted a glass of champagne from the hostess, temporarily reveling in the luxuries of the civilized world he was grateful to be a part of again.

As he idly leafed through the pages of the current issue of GQ, Robert let his mind wander back to the contrast between the material comforts of this society and the primitive crudeness of his Na Pali existence during the past couple of months, and he wondered at his own heretofore unknown ability to adapt. The adventure hadn't been what he expected, for sure. But it had provided an exercise in survival and a rich lode of metaphysical teachings. He was yet to realize the depth of personality change he had undergone. Fort now he was just glad to be wearing clean clothes, sipping champagne and listening to a funky beat. The flight was smooth and they landed at LAX just after 5:30. Robert was among the first passengers to enter Arrivals and the sight of his mom's dimpled grin was like a reward. They embraced and she tousled his head with amused reproach for his unkempt locks, complimenting him on his deep tan.

"You look heavy enough, I must say, although I think you've lost a little weight. And you look older, too."

"Do you think so, Mom? I haven't taken a good look at myself in a mirror since I lost my gear, you know! Always wanted to be leaner, meaner and older-looking you know!" He winked and punched her lightly on one shoulder as she unlocked the passenger side of the Jag for him.

"Well, you got your wish, Robby. Now, where to?" She laughed that silvery tinkle that he loved, and added, "I ask this while hoping desperately you'll say to the barbershop, of course!"

"That'll wait for a day or two, Mom. Let's head for home."

Lillian Radcliffe navigated out of the parking lot and into late afternoon traffic. It was bumper to bumper, as usual, and for the first time since he walked off Na Pali Robert felt a twinge of distaste. Thousands of cars were creeping along in the smoggy late afternoon haze, trying to get home from work. It felt like a person could make better time strolling the miles on foot! To pass the time, Robert fuddled with the radio dial and tried to pick up the aerial road report channel.

There had been a few fender benders, as usual. One real bad pileup on the Santa Monica freeway had killed one passenger and left the driver in critical. The news reported a shooting last night in Chinatown which had killed a policeman and a detective. A group of punk kids had died together in an overdose of uncut smack. *"Welcome to the real world, Robert,"* sneered his sarcastic inner voice.

Disgusted and discouraged, he inserted a Lionel Richie tape into the stereo and smiled at his mother, tapping his fingers absently to the music as they inched their way home.

***

23

Robert's desk was slacked with travel folders and school books, just as he'd left it. His clothes were pulled out of the closet and strewn around, silent witnesses to his indecision of packing. It seemed like he'd made this mess only yesterday but it felt like he hadn't been home for a year. And for the first time in his life he wished he hadn't forbidden his mother to stay out of his room. If he hadn't been so adamant about preserving his privacy she might have cleaned this mess up while he was gone!

He got a coke from the fridge and mentally gave thanks that his mom had gone to a meeting of her botanical circle, and his dad wouldn't be home until later. It gave him some time to wind down from the trip home and get used to being here again. Tonight, he knew they would ply him with questions. He needed time to reflect on exactly what to tell them about his trip.

Flipping the top off his coke, he ignored the mess and slumped into his favorite beanbag chair. Picking up the remote control on his TV he activated it with a familiar time-worn movement. A popular police show was playing another psycho-drama pitting the good guys against the bad guys. He changed channels. A sitcom he never cared for was on. He changed again and again until he found an old John Wayne western. He settled into his chair and picked up on the action.

His phone rang just as the argument in the bar was building up to a good fight. He loved the stunt work in those old western movie brawls.

"Rob, that you?" It was Larry. "Where in hell have you been? Your mom called me and said you were coming back today. She said you lost all your gear and got stranded in a remote area of some pacific island. What is the skinny, Man?" he asked.

"Hi Larry. How did your summer go?"

He ignored the question.

"The usual stuff. The usual people. How come you never wrote me a word? I mean, nearly three months without so much as a postcard! You promised you'd keep in touch, Man. We all thought you'd been kidnapped or murdered or something!"

"Do you want the long version or the capsulated account?" Robert responded dryly.

"Don't get sarcastic with me, chum! Tessa was worried out of her mind. She must have called your mother 10 times a day for the past two months, asking if your folks had heard from you yet. She's been driving us crazy man. Didn't your mom tell you?"

"Nope. She picked me up at the airport and dropped me at the house. Traffic was bitchin' and we got home late, so she tore off to her meeting right away. We really haven't had a chance to talk."

"Well, I'm waiting to hear what happened that was so friggin, important you couldn't send one measly postcard all summer long. You know, Tessa was so hysterical that Vickie made me call all the hospitals and police stations in Hawaii to ask if you were an accident victim or something like that. I can't believe your mother never told you!"

Same old Larry; always hitting the panic button and blaming it on somebody else.

"Okay, Larry, cool it. I'm alive and well. I did lose my backpack containing everything I owned. It was no big deal. I camped out with a friend in a rain forest area on Kauai and the summer passed so fast I almost forgot to come home. That's the short version. If you want anything longer, you'll have to catch me in a more talkative mood. I'm trying to watch an old John Wayne flick now. Signing off. Talk to ya *manana*!"

"Wait! How come you didn't write?"

"They forgot to plant mailboxes on that mountain, dummy. Over and out!" He hung up the phone before Larry could say anything more. The phone rang again almost immediately.

"Hey, Rob. You hung up so fast I didn't get a chance to tell you why I called. How about a game of tennis tomorrow and lunch at the club? I've got a court for 10 o'clock."

"Singles or doubles?"

"Singles. I didn't think you'd want to spill your guts in front of the girls and I warn you, I want to hear all about your trip over lunch!"

"Okay, you're on. See you at 10. Now back to my movie. Goodnight!"

This time he hung up the phone and then un-jacked it from the wall. Somehow, he just wasn't in the mood to be popular tonight. His mom and dad came home within minutes of each other, at around nine. For one reason or another, no one had eaten dinner, so his mom made some scrambled eggs and they all sat together in the kitchen, trading stories 'til bedtime.

Robert decided to stick to his long distance version of the story, and told it pretty much as it was except for not identifying Alopaka as a Menehune, and without mentioning the magical teachings. He also omitted the cave story in its entirety, preferring to risk being admonished for his carelessness in letting his backpack be swept into the sea than to scare his parents out of their wits with the thought that he might have died in a mountain fall.

In turn, he was glad to know his mom had contacted the issuer of the lost traveler's checks and put in a claim for refund of all unused checks. Ditto the airline return ticket. It would all take about ninety days, but the money would be refunded. His dad teased that losing all your documents was a cheap way to travel. His 10-week vacation had hardly cost them a thing. Then they smiled and assured him that the value of the travelers checks was his, used or not, and he would receive the refund money when it came.

Dad suggested he bank it for his next important project. So, it was two calm, unalarmed parents that Robert bid goodnight at midnight, as jetlag finally hit him and he headed for his room. He wasn't in the habit of fibbing to his folks, had never seen the need before, but this time he was glad he had. After all, the adventure was past and the only thing the truth would do would alarm them needlessly and alter their faith in his competency in the future.

***

24

The tennis match was more interesting than Robert had anticipated. For one thing, he had not only become leaner as a result of his summer's exercise and diet, but also more physically coordinated. Previously the stronger player, Larry now found himself equaled by Robert's speed and strength. Then, too, there was the Mana. As the ball lobbed back and forth hypnotically, Robert wondered idly if he could direct its course, and found that with a little practice he could push the ball around as easily as he had pushed the little cloud.

He would intentionally stand in the wrong place when Larry served, and make the ball come to him. As the ball began to do things contrary to the laws of physics, Larry became confused, then flushed and upset. Tossing the ball into a far corner, he brought a new one into play. Seeing this, Robert quickly decided to play it straight before Larry got wise to what was happening. Then he let Larry beat him, to cover his embarrassment at having played unfair with him.

"That was one weird game, Rob! For a while there it seemed as though the ball had a mind of its own! Really weird." He clapped his friend on the shoulder and said. "What do you want to do first, shower or eat?"

"Shower. I'm all sweaty."

They headed for the locker room together. As they combed their hair after changing into cotton pants and tees, Larry noticed the mass of dark curls.

"You starting a new fashion for hair or something?"

Larry joked. "Looks like you're trying to bring back the hippie look!"

"Man. Just didn't have time to get it cut before I came back."

"Well, if you don't get to the barber today, you'll have to start wearing it in a ponytail. Don't think Tessa is going to like the competition."

"You're right. I'll go in and see George in the salon right after lunch and see if he can give me a little trim."

After they'd been seated at a terrace table the waiter came up to take their order. "Perrier and a garden salad, please. No dressing," said Robert.

Larry raised an inquiring eyebrow and followed with, "Deluxe mushroom burger with cottage fries and a light beer." As soon as the waiter had departed, Larry laughed. "Man, you're eating habits have sure changed." He eyed Robert critically. "So, we observe that you are leaner and stronger, your hair is longer, your skin is browner and you eat like a rabbit nowadays. What else would you like to tell me about your trip?"

"There's really not much to tell."

"Not much to tell? You've been gone 10 weeks, or haven't you noticed? You must have done something in 10 weeks. Where all did you go? Did you meet any pretty faces... do a little dating, you know?"

"Nope. No bikini watching, no dates. Not a girl in sight." He watched his friend's expression change to one of total disbelief. "Had an interesting experience, though. Want to hear about it, although it doesn't involve wild parties or girls?"

"Wait a minute," Larry interrupted. "Am I wrong' or did you go to Kauai? I got a postcard from you the day you arrived, and it had a picture of Spouting Horn. What hotel did you stay at where there was no girls?"

"Yes, I did fly to Kauai. Those postcards I sent out from the airport were the only batch I had a chance to send, because after that I went climbing in a state park wilderness area and left civilization behind me for the next nine weeks."

"You can't be serious! You spent the whole time there in the jungle?"

"Jungle, rain forest, seashore, reefs, extinct volcanic pinnacles... I saw it all. The area is called the Na Pali Coast. It is remote, magnificent and still virgin land. It covers the entire northern end of the island and there are no roads through it, only trails made by deer or wild boar."

"Wow! Larry tried to sound impressed, but the eagerness faded from his eyes and Robert knew this type of adventure held no interest for his friend. He decided to change the subject.

"So! How've you been getting along with Vickie this summer? I remember you two weren't sure if you were going to take a rest from each other and spend the summer dating a variety of people?" Having thus pushed the right button, his friend rewarded him with a steady stream of talk about girls and dating and romance. Robert wondered if his hormones were ever going to start working overtime like Larry's. He hoped not. His friend either spent his time dating girls or fantasizing about them. This didn't make for very good company. He daydreamed and picked at his salad while Larry babbled on.

"Rob, Rob! Hey!" Larry was passing his hand back

and forth past Robert's eyes. "You asleep? Jet lag, I'll bet. Anyway, what do you say?"

"Sorry. Say to what?"

"To our getting together with the girls and going to Jellybeans tonight? I hear they've got a really good group playing there this week."

"Sure, why not? I'll Call Tessa when I get home."

"Why not call from here? We can ask the waiter to bring over a phone. This way we'll know right now whether they want to go or not."

"Okay, whatever you say."

He was reluctant to call Tessa and go through the "why didn't you write?" routine with her, too... much less with Vickie tonight, but he had to get it over with sooner or later. Larry called Vickie first, and got an excited acceptance.

Tessa sounded cool. Perhaps a little indifferent. The conversation was awkward. Robert issued the invitation and she hesitated.

"Listen, Tess, if you've found someone else while I was away, I'll understand, just say so... don't hem and haw at me like that."

"Oh, Robert." She sounded exasperated. "It's not that. I'm just disappointed. I thought you didn't care for me anymore when you didn't bother to write."

"Oh. Then you must have thought I didn't care for my parents or best friend, Larry, anymore, either. I understand you hounded everybody to death while I was away."

A sudden dial tone told him she'd hung up. To hell with her. Let her cool off and then maybe we'll get together. He was actually glad that she reacted badly. It gave him an excuse to avoid her for now.

"Larry," he said as he hung up the phone. "There's been a change of plan. We'll have to go alone. Tessa hung up on me. I don't know what her problem is, but I don't want to deal with it now."

Larry nodded. Women troubles were one thing he understood.

"Okay, buddy, it'll be boy's night out!" He picked up the phone again and told Vickie the date was off because Tessa had hung up on Rob. She protested that she'd talk to Tess and get her to go. But Larry assured her Rob was in no mood to go out with her now. She had no choice but to acquiesce.

***

25

After dinner, Larry came by for Rob and they played video games in the rumpus room to kill some time. They left for Jellybeans at 9. The place was jammed when they got there. It was Saturday night and, as one of the more popular yuppie hangouts in the area, the band was already playing to a standing-room-only crowd.

"Jeez, I'm glad we didn't bring the girls," shouted Larry over the deafening amplification of the band. "Looks like there's no place to sit!"

Robert peered into the darkness.

"Wait here," he shouted back. "I'll scout the room and see if there's any place we can sit."

"Okay," hollered Larry. "If I'm not here when you get back, look for me on the dance floor."

Robert nodded and weaved his way through the crowd, circling the dance floor first, then winding through the vast fabled area beyond. He knew the club well. He'd been coming here since he was seventeen. But this time the place was different, and he didn't like the change. "My God," he thought, "I can read everybody's thoughts!" Worse, he could also feel their emotions. The depth of anger, frustration, stress, insecurity and aggression hit him almost with the ferocity of a physical blow.

He tried to shut them out, to turn off the reception, but he could not.

Telepathic fragments of thought wafted into his brain as he passed the tables. *"I knew I shouldn't have dated you, you clumsy bastard. Look, you just spilled your drink all over the table cloth and down my leg!"* thought a pretty blonde with frizzy hair as she said, "Oh, Dave. Let me help you wipe that up." *"You think you can fool me, you slut! I know you are playing up to my best friend behind my back,"* snarled a tall boy internally as he smiled and said, "So, Trisha, what have you been doing with yourself all week?"

"You jerk. I'll get you for what you have done. You pretend to be a friend, but your uncle told me you didn't want him to hire me this summer in his lumber yard," threatened a red-haired youth internally as he looked up at a new arrival and his date to say, "Gosh, I'm sorry, Jeb. Like to have you sit with us, but we're meeting another couple here and we have to save these seats for them."

"Stop! Stop, stop, stop..." Robert screamed silently. "You're driving me crazy"

"You are full of it, as usual," accused a pretty brunette as she stood to receive the effusive greeting of another girl, squealing, "Jacquie! How long has it been!? So exciting to see you!"

He wanted to plug up his ears and run from this place as fast as he could.

"Hello, Rob. Long time no see."

At first he thought he was hearing it telepathically again.

"Rob?"

The voice persisted. He turned around.

"Oh, Donna! Excuse me. It's hard to hear anything in here" he said. "Don't I wish" He thought. "How've you been? And how's Gerry?"

"Same old life, same loveable Gerry. He's around here somewhere," she said with a wide smile.

"All guys are jerks and sex fiends," she thought, *"including you. Poor Tessa's been waiting to hear from you all summer, when she could have been dating other guys. And I, for one, am going to tell her I saw you here!"*

"Are you alone?" she inquired sweetly.

"Yes. And no. Excuse me," he replied as he pretended to see someone he had to talk to and pushed past her and onto the crowded dance floor. He elbowed his way through the dancing couples, humming to himself to block out any further intrusive dialogue and made for the glowing red EXIT sign on a side a door.

Outside he felt better. The sky was black, as usual. No delicate starlight could ever twinkle through this dense blanket of smog. He shoved his hands deep in his pockets and went for a stroll behind the club.

Suddenly he sensed a presence and sidestepped just in time to avoid tripping over a bum who was curled up in a fetal position, sleeping beside the garbage bins, drunk or stoned. The figure continued to sleep as Robert moved around him and walked on. Suddenly he decided to get out of here.

He felt the need of a nice, long drive. He longed to get out of the city and away from the smog to where he could see the stars. Returning to the EXIT door, which he had left off the latch, he reentered the club and almost immediately spotted Larry on the dance floor. In two strides he was at his friend's side. "Larry, listen, I need to borrow your car. Can you lend me the keys and catch a ride back with Donna and Gerry, or someone?"

Larry was having too good a time dancing with some tiny little chick with long black hair and almond eyes to give Robert the usual third degree.

"Sure, Rob. I think I can persuade Susie, here, to give me a lift home. Right, babe?" The Asian girl giggled and nodded, as Larry fished for the valet ticket in his jeans and handed it to his friend. "Just park it in the street, Rob, and leave the keys under the mat. I'll pick it up sometime tomorrow."

Robert drove out to the Valley, parked, and sat for a long time. Alone with his thoughts. Not even aware what a departure from normal it was for him to shut off the radio. He let the Mana flow through him as it had on the mountaintop, it filled him and nourished his spirit, and he rode it to the moon, while his physical body sat and waited in the car. He finally got home to a sleeping household at four in the morning.

***

26

Tessa dropped by on Sunday, full of contrition and apologies.

"That stupid Donna called me this morning to tell me you were out howling at Jellybean's last night, as if I didn't know. She must've thought she'd cause trouble. But it backfired on her. I told her you'd asked me and I couldn't go!"

Robert looked at her. He was still afraid of the third degree and feeling defensive about it. Sure enough, she voiced his worst fear.

"Rob, I was so upset at your neglect of me this summer. I was sure you didn't want to be my steady anymore. I was out of my mind when you disappeared like that without a trace." She clung to him. He wondered vaguely why the perfume of her hair didn't stir any emotion in him anymore, but his arms went around her waist, automatically. "Please don't do that to me again, Rob! Promise?"

He calmed her down and invited her to a movie that night. Things calmed down after that. The days passed uneventfully. Robert cleaned out his closets and threw away what seemed like tons of his childish toys. He wondered why he had kept this junk around for so many years. He guessed it had something to do with not being ready to grow up until now. Some of his friends were still on vacation while others were rushing around with last-minute preparations to go away to college.

For Robert this was no big deal. He was enrolled in

UCLA with a fairly light academic fall schedule. In fact, the most challenging thing on his agenda was finding a part-time job. Not that his parents were pressuring him. It was just something he wanted to do. When his closet was reorganized, Robert spread out his academic guide and tried to concentrate on selecting his courses for fall. Eventually, he forgot everything else in his single-minded pursuit of a curriculum. Larry called, day after day. Robert made excuses, day after day.

"What's the matter with you, Rob?

"Nothing, Larry. I just have a lot to do, that's all."

"Listen. You're not yourself since you came back from Hawaii. My mom knows a good shrink. Very progressive and easy to relate to. I can give you his name."

Alopaka warned me about that, he thought.

"Thanks, Larry, but I'm not off my rocker yet"

"Well, what's wrong with you' bud?"

"Maybe I'm just growing up!" he snapped sarcastically and added, "Talk to you later," before he hung up. For the next 10 days, he kept pretty much to himself. Every time he ran into a men, it was the same old intrusive questioning. He couldn't handle that.

He drove to the beach and went for swims in the chilly water, and he missed Hawaii. He chatted with the water sprites, the tree sprites and other friendly spirits and it was a relief to converse with beings whose inner thoughts held no contradictions or surprises. The sprites were simple and honest in their communication, and he grew to love his encounters with them. His parents began looking at him oddly trying to guess what was wrong. Although he could read their thoughts, he made no attempt to explain. How could he explain without being thought insane?

***

27

It was nearly mid-September and for three days weather forecasters had been broadcasting toxic smog warnings. As if that were not bad enough, Southern California was suffering a heat wave and people with respiratory problems were falling prey to the combination. It seemed that the entire Los Angeles area was populated with irrationally irritated people especially on the freeways. A sense of mounting hysteria was in the air.

On this third day the freeway was jammed bumper to bumper as usual, at seven in the morning as everyone rushed to work and school. The aerial traffic report station cited several fender benders and a couple of major pileups ahead. So what else was new?

Robert realized he would be late for his first class, but since there was nothing he could do about it, he relaxed in the comfortable bucket seat and switched to a music station. Wedged between a big black Buick in front and a white Mustang convertible in back, a pickup truck to the left and a VIA bug to the right, he crept along, a few yards at a time. He wondered if anybody had ever just left their car in the traffic jam and walked? Probably not. Nobody walked in Los Angeles. It would be considered abnormal.

He wiped the sweat from his forehead and turned up the air, wondering if he could successfully levitate the

the flow by pushing. And by now people in back of him were driving their cars around, shouting obscenities as they passed. The driver of the white Mustang tried to back up and go around the FIX7, as well, but there was no room. So he got out of his car and stormed up to the driver's window. He was a big stocky man with a ruddy face and thin red hair.

"Can you push this damned thing off the freeway?" His falsetto voice somehow didn't match his appearance. Watery blue eyes protruded from a flabby face and his shirt was soaked with sweat. He reeked of B.O.

"Sorry, Mister. We're doing what we can. I don't like this any more than you do," Robert replied.

"What you're doing is not enough!" he yelled. "Get this junk heap out of my way, or..." he finished his sentence with a kick to the door.

"Hey, Mister, watch what you're doing. You've made a dent there. I hope you're insured." Ral wiped his face with an arm as he spoke, and long streaks of black smeared his skin.

"Insurance my foot! Get this thing out of the way, I said!" The man kicked at the door again, his face turning purple and ugly as he screeched the command.

Robert felt a shiver of foreboding run up his spine. This guy was a nut case. There would be trouble, he felt sure of it.

"Please, Mister," begged Robert in an urgent attempt to diffuse the situation, "try to understand. We are doing everything we can, and the car won't start. Are you willing to help us stop oncoming traffic so we can push it over to the shoulder?"

The big man took this last remark as a challenge

rather than as the plea for assistance that it was intended to be. The look on his face was dangerous. "Get out of that car, you young punk! I'm not going to take that kind of lip from a young pup like you!" As the man reached for the door handle of the RX7, Ral sprang into action, leaping between the bully and the car door to forestall his obvious intention of yanking Robert out onto the pavement.

"Get out of my way, you goddamned pansy-assed kid!" snarled the big man, as he reached for Ral's jacket collar. Ral lost it. He swung at his captor and hit him with a smashing blow to his flabby gut. "Get your hands off me, you creep!" The man gasped and let go, then reached into his pants pocket. His fury was beyond control and his eyes shone with malignant light. The hand came out with something black and shiny in it.

My God, a gun! I have to stop him! A split second before he heard the shot, Robert lifted the latch and threw his weight against the car door so that it opened with enough force to knock the man out of the way. Knocked off balance by the blow, the revolver fell from the man's hand and rolled under passing cars on the pavement.

Traffic stopped to look. They sensed a sensational event here, and they forgot all about their rush to get to work in their eagerness to be spectators to it. A couple of college football types ran up and helped Robert pin the big man down and hold him there. Relieved of the need to control the big man, he looked around for his friend and found him face down on the pavement in an awkward Pose.

Oh no! Please! Not Ral! He prayed silently as he

knelt by his fallen friend. Turning him over, he lifted Ral's upper body and cradled it in his arms. The eyes were closed and the skin was ashen. Both hands were pressed to his chest to block the flow of blood. A small crowd of people had left their cars and gathered around with sad faces. Robert looked up.

"Somebody, please find a person with a car phone and call an ambulance. Quick, he's still alive!"

The crowd broke up and began walking down the lanes of stalled traffic, asking if anyone had a phone.

"Ral," Robert whispered. "Can you hear me? Everything's going to be okay. I've sent for an ambulance and I'll take care of you." He prayed an ambulance would arrive in time.

Ral opened his eyes. At first his gaze was unfocused but finally their eyes met. He opened his mouth but no sound came out. He winced with pain. Just then a man and woman rushed up and simultaneously announced they had called 911 and reported the shooting.

"Don't talk, Ral. The bullet might have punctured a lung. You need to conserve your strength. Just hang in there, buddy. The ambulance will soon be here."

Ral's mouth closed but Robert could read his thoughts.

"Rob, I don't think I'm going to make it. I think I'm done for!"

"No way! You're not going to die! Just hang in there, buddy. Help is on the way!" Robert pleaded urgently. But Ral was growing paler by the minute as the blood trickled out of him, and Robert could feel the life force draining out of him along with it. Where in hell is that ambulance?! The red stain on Ral's shirt was spreading fast. Robert tightened his grip' squeezing him harder as if to prevent his life force from escaping.

In the distance, he heard sirens, and looked down at his friend and said, "Here they come. Don't try to move. Don't try to speak. Just hold on, Ral, I'm with you." Ral's eyes opened again. He made a little burping sound and a trickle of blood dribbled out of his mouth. *"I can't hold on,"* he thought as Robert looked into his eyes. *"I've accepted the inevitability of my own death, Rob, you must accept it too!"*

He knows I can read his thoughts. Robert reacted with surprise. But why? Wasn't this the one friend he had once felt he could show his journal to?

"Ral, he replied aloud. "I know what's on your mind. I don't want to accept the inevitability of your death, because I don't want you to die! It's not fair!"

"So, since when do we come into this world with a guarantee that we are going to be treated fair? Some people live for decades as cripples or vegetables when they wish that someone would let them die. Others die when they have everything to live for. That's just the way it is. There is no reason, there is no justice, there is only acceptance of the unavoidable fact."

"You'd have made one helluva lawyer Ral," Robert said. "You've almost got me convinced in spite of myself. I don't want to lose you, though. It's hard to let go. Can't you stay with us long enough to let the doctors try to repair you?"

"Beyond repair," Ral thought. *"I can't hold on. Let me go. Accept the reality. Don't feel you are to blame. Tell my folks not to grieve. Death is not the end. It's just a passing. This body's had it, but I'll be back in a new*

one before long."

"How do you know that? Ral? Ral!" But there was no mental response. The eyes had gone blank and were staring up unseeingly at the sky. His life force had left him, blown out like the flame of a candle.

"Okay, folks, break it up. Break it up! C'mon, clear a path for the gurney please."

"Back to your cars, folks, this isn't a side show."

"Wheel that litter right through here, boys. We've got one civilian down. Hey! Get that fat guy into handcuffs and Mirandize him pronto, Officer Gonzales."

"What's your name son? Son? You can't just sit there. We have to take your friend. He's in good hands now. Joe! Help me pull his arms off this shooting victim so we can get a reading on his vital slats."

"Where's your car, Son?" Strong arms helped Robert to his feet. "We're going to have to take you back to the precinct for a statement." Robert was too choked up to speak. He merely pointed to his stalled RX7 while tears streamed down his face. "Was the victim known to you? Was he a passenger in your car, or was he riding with the perpetrator?" Roberts nodded his head up and down to the first question and negatively to the second, pointing across the lanes of traffic to the beautiful restored Desoto convertible parked on the shoulder.

"Sergeant, get across to that convertible on the shoulder and get an I.D. on this victim. Call a tow for three cars while you're at it, too. This guy's coming with us, and the perp has already been taken away."

***

28

He called his dad from the police station and the family lawyer was called in to hasten his release. Just the same, the questioning and statements took the rest of the morning and part of the afternoon. Everyone treated Robert as though he were ultra-fragile, and their thoughts were tender and considerate throughout the whole ordeal. Nevertheless, by the time he'd called AAA and gotten his car started he'd made a decision.

The first thing he did when he got home to his parent's empty house was call the airport and make a reservation to Hawaii. That night he sat his parents down and explained that he just couldn't hack this city living any more. He explained that the reason he had been so withdrawn since he returned from his trip was because he'd spent so much time living in rural simplicity that he couldn't make the readjustment to this society.

His parents were shocked. What, then, did he propose to do with the rest of his life? They demanded to know. "I have decided, with your cooperation and support, to return to the

island of Kauai. There I will enter the Kauai campus of the University of Hawaii and

Major in anthropology. When I complete my degree, it is my hope that my future employment will guarantee my choice to live with and study Micronesian and South Pacific races.

He paused to look at their astonished faces.

"Mom, Dad, look at it from my point of view. I have nothing in common any more with my old friends from high school. This summer was intended as a time for me to decide what I wanted to do with the rest of my life. Well, I've finally made up my mind."

His mother didn't look at all pleased.

"Wait, Mom! I know you'll miss me. But I'm not going to the end of the world. I want to spend my life working with native cultures in rural surroundings. No freeways, no supermarkets, no pop culture or drugs. You're both so busy these days. You with your career, Dad, and you with your volunteer groups, Mom. And you're hardly ever at home to be with me anyhow. I promise I'll come home for Christmas as often as I can."

He had his case so well presented that he really didn't leave them any argument. Caught, as they were, by the blow of Ralston's tragic death and overwhelmed with grief for the senior Howards, their good friends, they murmured few protests to a plan that would remove their own beloved son from this crazy society and keep him safe while he pursued anthropological studies in a tropical paradise.

He avoided calling Tessa to say goodbye. He wrote to her instead. He wrote to Larry and Donna, too, and sent a card and letter of bereavement to Ral's folks, quoting their son's last words in the hope it might bring them comfort. He would mail the letters from the airport. He asked his mom to pack and ship all his gear, glad now that he had culled all the useless junk from his room to make it easier for her.

His Dad had promised to cancel his enrollment at UCLA and transfer the refund on tuition, along with related paperwork, to the office of the registrar of UH Campus at Kauai. He also said he would phone the registrar to complete the arrangements and forward whatever fees were involved.

The next day was spent in last-minute arrangements, like selling his RX7 to a used car dealer for a fraction of what it was worth, and cleaning out his locker at UCLA, as well as converting his savings account into traveler's checks. Maybe he'd buy himself a motorcycle for transportation in Kauai. He'd have to play it by ear. Ral's last words had been, "Accept the reality." Robert's reality was that the lifestyle of this crazy, smoggy mega polis was not for him. For Robert, reality was a cool, green rainforest on a tropical island.

So when all is said and done, where is the real jungle? The real jungle is here, in LA, he thought to himself.

He thought of Alopaka. Somehow his jungle seemed so civilized and orderly, compared to this smoggy nightmare. Robert asked his dad for a lift to the airport the next morning. He hugged his mom and promised to write or call home every week. He tossed his luggage in the back seat and his dad drove faster than usual because they were late in getting on the road.

His plane for Honolulu would depart at 7:45 and he was afraid if he didn't check-in early, he'd get stuck in the smoking section. At 7:15 he was standing in the boarding lounge of United Air, sipping bitter black coffee from a paper cup. He remembered the strong rich flavor of the Kauai coffee beans and his mouth watered at the thought. He controlled his impatience. A five-hour flight to Honolulu, followed by another half hour flight to Kauai, and he'd be back where he belonged.

He decided to look Primo up during his layover and ask him if he wanted to send anything besides a hello to his granddad. Old Moki was going to fall down in surprise when he showed up to visit. He hoped he'd like the gift Robert had found for him. It was a special telescoping fishing rod and reel, the latest in high-tech equipment. The indifferent tiny voice of an airline employee announced his flight. He strolled down the ramp to the big 747, whistling softly to himself to the tune played by his new pocket cassette, which he'd bought to drown out the telepathic noise.

This time he had no backpack to wrestle with. He had carried adequate clothing, supplies and books along in a matched set of luggage provided by his mom. But he wouldn't see the luggage again until he reached Kauai. So, emotionally, the effect was of just walking away from it all. *"Free as a bird. Never look back!"* cautioned his inner voice.

He felt positively elated as he strapped himself into his seat. He was leaving an old, useless way of life and heading into a new era and a career that would give him a real feeling of purpose, a real reason for being on Earth.

***

29

If you get to Honolulu, you might find Primo still driving his SIDA taxi, and if you do he'll tell you where Robert Radcliffe's living now. Once he graduates he might be as far away as Bora Dora, Tahiti, Samoa or Palau. But if you fly to Kauai one day and drive up Hanalei way, you might want to look up Tutu's store. If

Robert's still on the Garden Isle, Tutu and Moki will know. And you'll be welcome there, whatever age you are, if you have an open mind and an open heart.

But don't forget to leave your frustrations at home in the closet. There's no place for such uncivilized feelings beyond the rainbow.

GLOSSARY OF HAWAIIAN WORDS

Note: Many Hawaiian words have more than one meaning depending upon placement of diacritical (pronunciation) marks. However, current browser technology does not facilitate universal and uniform application and utilization of Hawaiian diacritical by browser fonts and search engines. As a result, we have been unable to use them on this site.

Following are common meanings to some widely used Hawaiian Words:

Aa: rough, crumbling lava.
Ae: yes.
Ahupuaa: land division usually extending from the mountains to the sea.
Akamai: smart, clever.
Akua: god, goddess, spirit, ghost, devil, image, idol, corpse; divine, supernatural, godly.

Ala: a road, path, or trail.

Alii: a Hawaiian chief, Hawaiian royalty.

Aloha: love, affection, kindness. Also means both greetings and farewell.

Aole: no.

Aumakua: family or personal gods, deified ancestors who might assume the shape of, for example, a shark, owl, dog, hawk, plant, or cloud.

Hale: a house.

Haole: white person. Formerly any foreigner.

Hapa: a part, sometimes a half.

Hauoli: to rejoice. Hauoli Makahiki Hou: Happy New Year.

Heiau: an ancient Hawaiian temple.

Hele: to go, come, walk.

Holo: to run.

Hookipa: hospitality.

Huhu: angry.

Hui: a group, club, or assembly.

Hula: the dance of Hawaii.

Imu: underground oven.

Ipo: sweetheart.

Ipu: the bottle gourd used as a receptacle, dance rattle and drum.

Iwi: bone.

Ka: the definite article.

Kahuna: a priest, doctor, or other trained person of old Hawaii, endowed with special professional skills that often included the gift of prophecy or other supernatural powers.

Kai: the sea, saltwater.

Kalo: the taro plant from whose root poi is made.

Kamaaina: literally, a child of the soil, it refers to people who were born in the Islands or have lived in Hawaii for a long time.

Kanaka: originally a man or humanity in general, it is now used to denote a male Hawaiian or part-Hawaiian.

Kane: a man, a husband.

Kapa: also called tapa, a cloth made of beaten bark.

Kapu: taboo, keep out, prohibited, sacred.

Kapuna: grandparent, ancestor, elder.

Keiki: a child.

Kokua: help.

Kuleana: responsibility, concern, property.

Lanai: a porch, balcony or deck.

Lani: heaven, the sky.

Lauhala: the leaf of the hala or pandanus tree, widely used in Hawaiian handcrafts.

Lei: a garland of flowers.

Lokahi: unity, agreement, harmony.

Luau: Hawaiian feast. In the past the word for feast was paina.

Mahalo: thank you. Mahalo nui loa: thank you very much.

Makai: toward the sea.

Malihini: a newcomer to the Islands.

Mana: the spiritual power that the Hawaiians believed to inhabit all things and creatures.

Mauka: toward the mountains.

Mauna: mountain.

Mele: chant, song, anthem. Merry Christmas: Mele Kalikimaka.

Menehune: a legendary race of little people who worked at night building fish ponds, roads and temples.

Moana: the ocean.
Muumuu: a loose gown or dress.
Nani: beautiful.
Nui: big.
Oli: a chant that was not danced to.
Ono: delicious
Pahoehoe: smooth lava.
Pahu: drum.
Pali: a cliff, precipice.
Paniolo: a Hawaiian cowboy.
Pau: finished, done.
Puka: a hole.
Pupu: hors d'oeuvres
Wahine: a female, a woman, a wife.
Wai: fresh water, as opposed to saltwater, which is kai.
Wikiwiki: to hurry, hurry up.